rhythm of the chain

rhythm of the chain
YOUNG WRITERS EXPLORE TEAMWORK

**BY THE STUDENTS OF
ÁNIMO INGLEWOOD
CHARTER HIGH SCHOOL**

IN CONJUNCTION WITH 826LA
INTRODUCTION BY PHIL JACKSON

826LA

Rhythm of the Chain

Published June 2005 by 826LA

First Edition

826LA
SPARC Building
685 Venice Blvd.
Venice, CA 90291
(310) 305-8418
www.826la.org

Design: Michele Perez
Copy Editors: Sherri Schottlaender, Tami Mnoian
Photography: Anne Fishbein

Printed in Canada by WestCan P.G.

CONTENTS

It seems that there are always going to be caretakers of our youth. I'm one who has lived with a certain type of young man for the past thirty-seven years—professional basketball players. It has been my practice to give books to my players and make them read in front of the team to see how their reading skills have developed. The responsibility to have a continuing education for these men, caught in the world of the ever-young warrior athlete, has been part of my job because there is a time when they will have to enter the "real" world. While many of the athletes I have coached have been proficient readers and writers, some have had to struggle to comprehend the written word and have had little ability to write.

It was my chance opportunity to have Jim Hester as my teammate in college. Jim was struggling academically when he arrived at school from Davenport, Iowa. I became his friend and study-mate during that arduous first year of college, a year in which he became ineligible to play sports (so much for my skill as a tutor). He then had another year of ineligibility and lost his basketball scholarship, but he kept trying. Jim started making the grades and he got a football scholarship. He graduated from college and later became an NFL player, but perhaps his biggest accomplishment was when he got elected to the Board of Education in his hometown. Jim wanted the children in his community to get this important message: Don't miss out on the opportunities that education can bring.

As a sophomore in high school I had the good fortune to have Miss Turner as my English teacher. She saw that I had a great deal of passion about literature; she also saw that even though my writing had imagination, it didn't meet the standards necessary to effectively communicate what I wanted it to. Miss Turner was willing to work with me and use my love of the written word to help me become a better writer—and even though I have grave doubts about my ability to write, somehow in the past thirty years I have had five books published that proclaim me author or co-author. It is because of my desire to write well and my continuing love of the written word that my friend and former wife, June Jackson, got me interested in 826 Valencia. It was her love of editing and her passion for educating children that led to her volunteering as a tutor at 826 Valencia in San Francisco, an organization established by Dave Eggers.

For the past three years, June has been telling me about the great things that 826 Valencia is doing for inner-city kids in San Francisco, and I was glad that she'd found an outlet for her skills as nurturer and tutor. On a visit to San Francisco over Christmas this past year, June and I and two of our children went down to the storefront on Valencia to meet Dave; we spent the morning talking about the process of getting kids excited about writing. Dave asked me to assist in the opening of a similar space in L.A. called 826LA, as well as a joint venture he envisions undertaking with a school called Ánimo Inglewood. He explained to me how a book that reflects a unifying idea or topic can be written and published by students, and he asked if I might be interested in assisting with such a project for the Ánimo school.

I knew it was something I'd like to do, but what could I give these students that they could write about? I thought about the idea of teamwork, how to work as a group. I wondered how students at a school without a great emphasis on sports, but rather on academics, would react to writing about a topic that's so identified with athletics, but we decided that "teamwork" would be the book's topic.

> *Now this is the Law of the Jungle—*
> *as old and as true as the sky.*
> *And the Wolf that keeps it shall prosper,*
> *but the Wolf that breaks it must die.*
> *As the creeper that girdles the tree-trunk,*
> *the Law runneth forward and back,*
> *For the strength of the Pack is the Wolf,*
> *and the strength of the Wolf is the Pack.*
> — RUDYARD KIPLING

This is the excerpted poem that I gave the student editors of this book in late March, a few months after the project named Team Jackson was initiated at Ánimo Inglewood. I left for a trip to Australia, New Zealand, and the South Sea Islands, and when I came back the students were in their second and third rewrites, with the help of their tutors.

Perhaps I should have given the student writers this Kipling poem from *The Jungle Book* before the project got going—that might have given these pieces a few boundaries—but these are the stories that the students wanted and needed to tell. "Team Jackson" was just the catchword for the project: the project is about teams, teams that are families, teams that are groups of people, and teams that have bonded with these students and influenced their lives.

"There is a destiny that makes us brothers, no man goes his way alone. What I put into the life of others, will return unto its own." This anonymous rhyme is another poetic piece that I have given to the teams that I've coached over the past eighteen years. In reflecting upon this "destiny that makes us brothers," I believe that Ánimo Inglewood's writers have found what I really wanted them to explore. What is the fiber of our society that bonds us together? We live in a large metropolitan area that challenges us daily to find a thread of common material that can allow us to live together in peace. Inside these pages you will find stories that declare that bond—even through the horror of drive-by shootings, the heartache of debilitating disease, the tribal/cultural instincts to trust only "our" kind, and the cry for respect in a world of anonymity. These stories accurately reflect life in this incredibly diverse city. We seek peace and understanding as people living in a larger world as well, and that is the essence of these writings.

I want to thank the incredible teachers from Ánimo Inglewood, Annette Gonzalez, Allen Monroe II, and Melinda Viren, who have encouraged and labored with these writers; Ánimo's principal, Cristina de Jesus, and its founder, Steve Barr; and the parents who have sacrificed so that these young people can have the opportunity for an education that challenges and encourages them to be special. Thanks also to Pilar Perez, to the 826LA tutors, and to the editorial board who have given their time and expertise to making this book happen for the students.

Phil Jackson played professional basketball for fourteen years with the New York Knicks and the New Jersey Nets. He was a member of the Knicks' two championship teams. In 1982, after a year in business, Jackson began coaching and returned to the NBA as a coach in 1987. His NBA coaching career has been highlighted by nine championships; three with the LA Lakers and six with the Chicago Bulls. He is the father of five children. He has authored five books, including Sacred Hoop *and* The Last Season.

Quarter 1: The Locker Room

Are we a team?
Yes, Coach!
Do we want to win?
Yes, Coach!
Are we going to win?
Yes, Coach!

Everybody's goal should be the same
You don't go out and try to impress your name.
You pass to who is open, don't take every shot
And make sure you keep your eyes on the clock.

I want us to score at least seventy points, and I want them to be equaled out
I don't want Reggie making all seventy, he is not the only person on
This team, so please, you guys, play as a we.

Let's put our hands and heads together now, let's win as a team,
Give each other support, cheer each other on. You guys are also
Fans, do we understand?

Coach: Contradicting Thoughts

I remember when Reggie was only seven, man, when that boy
Threw up the ball, he made it look like it was floating in
Heaven.
I just had to have him on my team, but I didn't realize he
Did not know how to be a we. The name on the front is
Way more important than the name on the back. How do

I get him to see that?
Coaches would die to have a boy like this on their team.
Am I wrong for not letting him play to his best ability?
I want people to know that he is the best, but I have to
Give the rest of the boys a chance to see that they are also capable.
Now, I just hope Reggie doesn't let me down.
If he does not play as part of a team tonight
I am going to have to let him go, and tell him he is
Not coachable.

Half-Time: Reggie and Donald

Man, I am sick of this. How am I supposed to get recruited
When our team is always losing?
I can go out there and make all them points,
But no, no, Coach doesn't want that, it would give him a heart attack.

Reggie, what did Coach say? We have to have the same goal to be able
To work as a team. Have you ever really thought about what that means?
It means you have to take a little beating, and you have to sacrifice.
Reggie, you are only as good as clumsy Paul, and yes, he is our weakest
link.
So stop all the I'm this and I'm that, and play with us and
Cut yourself some slack.

I got you, but it's hard. At my old school, I was averaging thirty points a
Game, and at this school I want to do the same. Man, this team mess is
Lame. I am used to throwing up the ball when I get a chance but you're
Telling me I have to let go of that. You got me super twisted
In a huge way. My name is Reggie. You're lookin' at the next MJ.

Reggie, do what you got to do, do what you feel is right. But when
You're not at our game tomorrow night because Coach is through
Don't say I didn't try to tell you.

Game Over: Coach and Reggie

Coach, how you like them points I was putting up?

Enough, Reggie, enough. You are off this team until you can

Show me what being a team really means.

But Coach, we won the game. What's the big deal?

No, Reggie, you won the game. We did not win a thing.
How many times did I tell you that you have to play
As a team? A team will win together, and a team will lose
Together, but the way you're going, you won't get anything accomplished
Except for what is happening so far. Reggie you're not on this team anymore.

Coach, I made fifty points out of the sixty that we had. What's so
wrong with that?

Let me break it down. You had fifty, which means the team only
Averaged ten. How does that sound? It doesn't sound like a win.
Reggie, I am through arguing with you. I made up my mind and
I am not changing it until you decide you can be a we instead
Of an I. I am through talking now, good-bye.

Outside: Donald and Reggie

You're off the team, aren't you?

Yeah, man, and I can't understand why.

Well, until you learn the concept of a team, you and
Coach are never going to see eye-to-eye.

Oh well, man, I don't need a team, I am going to do it my way.
My name is Reggie. I am the next MJ.

College: Coach and Donald

So Donald, how have you been? With that four-year scholarship in ball
Your life can't be bad at all.

I am good, Coach, as good as I can be. But can you answer me this:
Whatever happened to Reggie?

You mean the next MJ? Well, I guess he is doing fine. Right now he is at
A community college playing ball.
No, I take that back, he is on the bench all the time.

Are you serious?

As serious as I can be. Did you notice how after he left we began to
Win, and win as a team? See, when you got that star player who wants
To make every point, you're not gonna make it anywhere. Just remember
That, boy.

Reggie: My Lesson

As I sit on the bench after playing for just one minute, I see what my
Old high school coach was talking about. So many scouts saw me play,
And I used to wonder why am I here today. I used to wonder why I am
Not yet in the NBA. I really used to see myself as the next MJ. I ask
Myself these questions no more, because I have found the answer, and I
Want you to hear it from the primary source. Instead of just me, I am
Part of a team. I lose with them, and I win with them, too.
Honestly, I am nothing without them, because without a team
What are you, seriously? I know who I am. I am not the next MJ.
My name is Reggie, but not just the I, I am now a we.

MY FAMILY IS MY FLOWER BED
DANIELA DOWELLS

People say I'll never 'mount to anything
These people from my past.

I was a single seed planted in an overflowing patch of weeds,
Drowning with these ignorant people and backstabbing friends.
The ones who smile in your face, then go around and talk behind your back.
"She's a brat."
"She's conceited."
"She's fake."
"She's just a child."
These comments are tearing at my roots!
And then there's that teacher
Who gave me a failing grade due to a mistaken race,
Until she saw my father's African American face.
You're probably thinking, how much can I take before I break?

These unforgivable actions will always be here and can never be erased.
To prevent decaying, this rose learned to grow thorns.

But these thorns are useless to me because I have my team:
My mother, my brother, my sister, my grandparents.
They helped me, raised me, and damn near built me.
"Mind your elders."
"Keep your game up."
"We always have your back."
"I love you, *we* love you."

My family built my respect towards others, my style unlike others, my
motivation, and my imagination.

Take a look at me now!
I went from a root in the ground to a full-grown rose,
High school student,
Honor roll,
Even writing in Phil Jackson's book.
NOW WHAT?!

You think I'm young and don't know much about life and still have a
long ways to go.
But I have reached my pinnacle of rising towards the sun.

Those of you who tried to put me down, all you did was strengthen my roots.

These weeds had only a positive effect on me because
My family, *my team*, was there for me, and that will always be a
permanent thing!

POWER TO THE PEOPLE
JENNIFER ANDERSON

The year was 1966. A child was innocently biking down a sidewalk in Oakland, California, when—BAM! He was struck down by a car and killed. The absence of a stop sign, a traffic light, or a crossing guard caused the death of this young man. What could the people in the neighborhood do to right this wrong? How could the community protect itself from future incidents like this? How could they protect innocent children?

The neighborhood banded together and changed Oakland's unresponsiveness to problems within the community. With intelligence and purpose, the community leaders reached out to their followers. This is how the Black Panthers Party was born.

The Black Panther Party was established in 1966 by Huey Newton, Bobby Seale, and group of other young African Americans who wanted to give back to and improve their community. They set out to make the neighborhoods of Oakland safe for all minorities, especially children. The group of politically active African Americans came together to improve their social and economic standing. They implemented breakfast programs, sickle cell testing, and protested the Vietnam War. They fought for equal rights and respect from law enforcement. Their mantra: Power to the people.

For more than a decade the Black Panther Party remained a strong force. The party disintegrated because of FBI infiltration, violent raids launched by law enforcement, and rising legal costs. Many people sacrificed and died for what they believed in, but due to the militant action against the party, their organization lost its momentum. In the late 1980s, a similarly minded group formed who stole the original party's name and image; they called themselves the New Black Panthers. They weren't affiliated with the original party and weren't as community-oriented. As the party's successors, they are useless. They spread negative propaganda about other racial groups and are sometimes considered to be a hate organization. Ideally, community organizations should work towards improving a society; they do not.

It's been more than thirty years since the Black Panthers were first established, and the world is still a dangerous place. Not too long ago in Inglewood, California, a mother took her second-grader to Darby Park to register for youth basketball and to pick up his well-deserved soccer trophy. Darby was his favorite park; she thought, why should the darkness of night make it any less lovable? He got in the car with his baby brother, ready to go home. His mother noticed another car beside them. It was filled with gang members with guns pointed at them. As his mother frantically tried to back up the car, gunfire erupted. She turned around to see her son's shirt drenched in blood: bullets from the Mac-90 struck the seven-year-old three times in the head, killing him instantly. Some of the fragments also struck his ten-month-old brother, who sat beside him; he was partially blinded in his left eye.

The boy was only in the second grade when he died. None of this young boy's dreams and aspirations would ever be fulfilled. His life was snuffed out. His community, church, and school were left to deal with this loss. Vigils and press conferences were held, but senseless acts of violence still continue today.

There is a contrast between the 1960s and now. Our world has significantly changed since the sixties. As a society we have become less and less unified, less willing to come together for a cause. What are we going to do about it? What is the African American community going to do about it? Clearly, the New Black Panther Party isn't the answer, and the old party is gone. People need to work together as a team to solve problems that arise. Communities can band together, like the original Black Panthers did, and influence each other. If we stay together, positive change can happen.

When I first started this project I had no idea how teamwork related to me. Through exploring the history of the Black Panther Party, I came to realize how important teamwork is. What they did had an impact on how I think and live. As an African American teenager, I feel that their efforts have influenced how I live by motivating me to always fight adversity and to expect respect from those I give respect to. The people who came before me fought for the rights I have today. I feel I owe it to them— it's my responsibility to take advantage of opportunities that come my way. If more of my peers felt this way, change could happen. It's possible as long as people put aside their differences and come together. The Black Panthers put up that stoplight; what will our generation's stoplight be?

THE MORENOS
JACKIE MORENO

It was a warm, sunny day, my cousin Alvaro's wedding day. Everyone in my family was there. All the boys and men—including my brothers Alex, Raul, and Ramiro—wore tuxedos. My sisters Connie, Patty, Gaby, Kimberly, and Maria wore tender pink dresses with small colorful flowers. My cousins and aunts wore purple, and some had dresses made out of soft silk. Everyone was prepared to see the happiest day of Alvaro's life.

The air was so fresh and clean that you never got tired of smelling it. The church was so tall, it looked like it could reach the sky. It was white and light pink and had a big cross on the top. Inside it was filled with flowers, in the aisles and around the altar. The flowers smelled like strawberries and peaches tingling inside your nose.

My cousin eagerly waited for his bride-to-be, Reyna, at the altar. His smile was as bright as the sunlight, and when you looked at him, you couldn't help but smile back. When the ceremony began, it was magnificent, everything in perfect order. First, the groomsmen and bridesmaids walked in two at a time. Then came Reyna. She had on a long white dress with a veil over her face. She moved with grace, slowly and calmly. Alvaro recited his vows, telling Reyna he would be there for better or for worse, in sickness and in health. Reyna recited the vows back to him. Afterwards, Alvaro and Reyna took pictures with my cousins outside the church.

I was talking to Gaby when suddenly I heard a loud crashing noise, like someone breaking a glass. It was my Uncle Rodrigo, Alvaro's father. He had a seizure and fell crashing against another uncle's car window. I could hear ladies screaming and crying from far away, but it sounded as if they were right next to me. I was aware of everything and everyone around me. At that moment, I no longer felt that the day was warm and beautiful. My cousins stared blankly, as if they didn't know what was happening. The groom ran to his dad and put his hand in his mouth so my uncle wouldn't swallow his tongue. Reyna was right there by his side. Their vows were already put into use minutes after they had recited them. My dad also ran to his brother, looking as if someone had ripped out his heart.

An ambulance took my uncle to a hospital four blocks away from the church. We all knew that his drinking problem was going to catch up to him sooner or later, but no one expected it would be on the day of his son's wedding. The quick action of Alvaro and my dad saved his life.

Alvaro stayed at the hospital with his dad while Reyna went to the reception with the guests. The reception was awkward—people wanted to be with my Uncle Rodrigo and Alvaro, but instead kept Reyna company. It was difficult to concentrate on only one of them. My dad went to the hospital with some of my brothers, and the rest of my brothers and sisters went to the reception. When Alvaro finally got to the reception, he let everyone know that my uncle Rodrigo was doing well. Still, nothing went as planned for the rest of the day. People didn't want to eat their food, and the bride and groom did not continue to take pictures as arranged. Alvaro's mind was with his dad even though he wanted to be with Reyna at the same time.

My brothers and sisters couldn't believe what had happened, and they tried to comfort my parents and each other. I thought of my parents differently as well. I had never seen my parents so worried, especially my dad. He wanted to be with his brother and find out about his situation. I started thinking about my brothers and sisters. I was wondering, "Would I run to help my brothers or sisters?" I thought, "I would be worried and panicked, just like him." I put myself in my dad's situation and understood how he felt for the first time.

This incident affected everyone in my family. My uncle realized that drinking was not a solution to anything and he stopped, for his health and the family; even though the family had told him that before, he now believed it for himself. As for me, I learned that I need to cherish my family even more because you never know when something bad can happen. Now when I'm angry at my brothers and sisters, I think, "It's not worth it because if they were not here, I don't know how I would handle things."

There is no team better than my family. We are the Morenos.

THE DEATH OF A STAR
CHRISTINA STEWART

The printed word is a prisoner. It dwells in reality but runs free and wild in surrealism. The books scattered on the bookcase, waiting to be chosen—staring out windows racing skyward from the sidewalk. But then someone enters and the store bell sings a hopeful melody. The selected few open up and the words leap off the page, latching on to the reader, aware that they are that much closer to freedom. The bell sings once more, but this time a song of mournful good-byes for the prisoners left on the shelf, each crowded by its neighbors, yearning to be liberated.

In the same sense, a team is also a prison; it confines its players to a set of rules and regulations, sworn to the motto, "All for one and one for all." Humans strive for independence, which often conflicts with the idea of teamwork. A team is made up of individuals who have individual egos. Every team has its star, and a star's intent is to shine. The idea of an organized, well-balanced team forces the star to sacrifice much of his true ability in order to become one with the team.

Is teamwork more detrimental than beneficial to individuals? By having to "give a little to get a little," we curb our true ability to excel. Each player is a slave to the team's rule book, restrained by shackles of togetherness and unity. What good, after all, are gifts never opened, simply left under the Christmas tree to perish and be consumed by dust? A star holding back his talents is like trying to submerge a ball underwater—you can't! Immediately the ball rebels against the pressure; it shoots violently to the surface. The player, in a sense, is an artist—the ball is his paintbrush and the hardwood his canvas. By stifling the individual, the coach is confiscating the painter's tool.

Offensively, the individual is a convict, condemned to the playbook. Every movement is planned out, every dribble is predicted, every pass anticipated, and every execution premeditated. Oh, the agony of monotony! The star longs to be sporadic, unpredictable. He aches for liberation, the freedom to break outside his fixed territory. The second the coach diverts his attention elsewhere—perhaps stealing a glance at the score or devising yet another systematic play to drive to the basket—the star beams! He draws in a fresh breath of freedom and basks in his deliverance. When the coach looks back, he is alarmed by the chaos. He signals desperately for a time-out. The team retreats to their base and prepares a new play, a new plan of attack to suppress the individual.

Defensively, the star must hide behind a shield—his team—ducking and dodging the bullets exploding from the half-court line. In a 2-3 zone, the team uses its players' efforts to hide their weaknesses; the fault lies in the post players. The individual's true desire is to take his opponent head-on and dominate the entire court—defensively and offensively. The star is able to exert his defensive abilities to help the team as well as himself. The star's team, though, crowds his spotlight, dims his light, curtails his shine.

Conventional theories of teamwork hinder the benefits of individualism; however, individualism is everyone's secret desire. Playing on a basketball team tests character, patience, and true desire. A basketball team has one mission and one mission only—to push the ball down the court, put it in the net, and win the game. The individual's goal, however, is to boost his personal statistics. This breeds healthy competition within the team, eventually leading to a stronger performance. Teamwork causes the individual to surrender his utmost abilities to unite with the group. Ultimately, little is gained, while much is lost. As the final buzzer rings, the team celebrates their hard-earned victory, but mourns the death of their star.

OUR FAMILY PORTRAIT
SHAWNA STEPHENS

From the second of December

Those two years, I remember

Traveling from foster home to foster home

My mother and father, I've never known

But special prayers have been bestowed upon me

From the adoption agencies, I became free

To live with new parents in a new home

Where I could grow and come into my own

Day after day, I enjoyed going to school to learn

To get an education, for that I have yearned

From preschool to seventh, I advanced with honors

Eighth grade was difficult, but I graduated a scholar

Hard work and dedication in all things that I do

Just to walk across the stage, proud, and not see you

You, as in my new family, the ones that I care for

The ones that I thought cared for me too

But although you hurt me, I had to stay strong

I struggled with obstacles, but still moved on

My parents want me to seek a higher education

But I'm tired of school and all its frustrations

I spent years trying to find what I want to be

Striving to be a wedding planner is what makes me happy

They think school's what I need, but I don't agree

What I want you to see is that I strive for the best

Nothing but greatness and excellence

That's what I want, that's what I am

And not to defy you, mom and dad, but that's where I stand

I need to succeed because you don't accept me

I feel as if I'm distant, not a "true" part of your family

Like there's this family portrait, and I'm not in it

Though I wouldn't be where I am if it weren't for you

Still I don't understand many things you do

Why you didn't come to my graduation

But you're the ones who pushed me to get there

You don't support the career that I want for the future

It's as if you don't care

Those are the things that hurt me and make me cry

But I've taken those things in and have swallowed my pride

Now I understand the reason I try

But I also need you to understand why

I try because I want for us to be a "true" family

And a "true" family sticks together in times of need

We need each other

We need to stand by and support one another

I'm here for you and you're there for me

That's my impression of what a "true" family should be.

The portrait of our family

It was the worst day of my life
And it wasn't even my plight
Something so simple, but illegal
Turns into something so lethal

Ordered to stop in between those two long yellow lines
Obviously the young boy did not hear his father's cries
We reached our destination and came to a stop
The young boy, however, did not

He kept running towards his own destination
Running seemingly forever with no resignation

His father is still yelling, while I'm silent
Knees shaking, internally sobbing
People watching, not knowing what to say
Wishing it were a dream and not a real twenty-four-hour day

A car comes to a screeching halt
The scene I'm witnessing must have a fault
I see the young boy fall flat on his back
Taste, smell, feeling, and hearing are the senses I lack
My sight is the sense that I do retain
Wishing that all the others I would soon regain

The sight of the young boy with his back on the ground
Leaves me with questions whose answers will never be found
Why didn't he stop? Why'd he keep running?
What just happened here? A few moments ago the boy was just beaming
Please tell me I'm asleep and vividly dreaming

Then the unthinkable happens
The boy starts to get up
As if by an angel he had been touched
All of my worst thoughts were then dismissed
For the car had just barely missed

Then questions flooded my mind again
What made the boy fall back? And many more with answers no one
would send
Then I finally realized that I didn't even care
For the young boy was alive
He was standing there

So you may be wondering why this young boy's plight
Happens to be the worst day of my life
For this young boy could not be replaced by any other
Because this young boy is my brother

Epilogue

This could happen to anyone's family, even yours. My best advice would
be to cherish your family and do anything it takes to keep them safe and
out of harm's way, even if you're doing something as simple as walking
across the street at the designated stops for pedestrians.

Looking back on this event in my life, it hits me: "I almost lost my
brother." Someone that I've known and loved for twelve years could be
gone. I always thought of us as the perfect family. We had a mother, a
father, a daughter, and a son. I always pictured that as right, and without
my brother, my parents' son there, it would have been wrong. I would
miss fighting and arguing with him. I would miss sharing my room with
him and fighting over whose night it was for the television. I wouldn't be
complete without him. I couldn't be complete without him.

I look at his second chance at life as being God's grace. When we
reached our destination, I was still terrified and couldn't speak, and my
father proceeded to yell and scream at my brother for not stopping. Tears
of fear ran down my brother's face, and they almost ran down mine, too. I
couldn't fathom why my father was yelling at him after something so life-
threatening had almost happened. Later on I realized that my father was
scared, just like I was scared, and just like my brother was scared. We
almost lost a piece of our family, a piece of our team.

MY DREAM TEAM: GIRLFRIENDS, FAMILY, HUSBAND
COURTNEY JOHNSON

Every little girl dreams of her wedding day. For as long as I can remember, I have been dreaming of mine. I have no doubts that it will be the most wonderful day of my life. Growing older, my dreams have become more elaborate. In my mind, I can see every detail of that day and I know that I am not there alone. As I close my eyes, I see my dream team and my wedding . . .

Beep, Beep, Beep, Beep, Beep! The alarm clock rings loud and clear. I awake from a sweet dream in which I was reliving meeting the love of my life. It had been love at first sight when I met Marcell Whan on Sunday, May 30, 2004. My friend Allison had made it all possible—or at least her cell phone did. He had been using her cell phone and accidentally dialed my number. We ended up talking until 2:00 A.M., other nights until 4:00 A.M. or even 7:00 A.M. We finally met one day when I tagged along to their weekly teen class. From that day on, our love grew rapidly.

"Wake up, ladies, it's time to get ready. Somebody call the hairdresser, wake the boys, call the chefs, pick up the dresses from the cleaners, and get pretty ladies! ASAP! It's my wedding day and nobody's lookin' ugly!" I cry out orders as I run down the hallway of the hotel knocking on everybody's door, even those who aren't part of my wedding.

This isn't just any day, it's *the* day, and I can't have any mistakes! Aris approaches me, wide awake, saying, "Courtney, I just got off the phone with the hairdresser, and she and her assistants are on the way, and Melissa is going to get the dresses from the cleaners." My friend Aris knows how to handle any situation.

Melissa, Jade, Allison, and Aris are my lovely bridesmaids. They are the backbone of this wedding, even though I've been driving them crazy. Melissa, aka Mel, is our "weird, goofy friend," but she is also a serious journalist. Jade is the "crazy, psychotic one" who models professionally.

Allison, aka Alli, is the "big mama" among us—she's a major film director. That leaves Aris, the "bookworm/lawyer." Though we've all been friends since high school, Aris and I have become best friends over the years. Today she is my maid of honor. We've all been through good times and hard times together, which has made our bond strong and unconditional; we're like sisters. That's why it's so important that my girls are in this with me today—they are holding me together like glue.

Allison is the most truthful of the group. She'll be honest about anything, even if it's something going wrong on your wedding day.

"Uh, Courtney . . . I have good news and bad news," she says. "The good news is that the boys are up and getting ready as we speak."

"And the bad news?" I ask.

"Bad news—Brian isn't here."

"And why is that bad news?" I ask slowly, squinting my eyes.

"Courtney . . . Brian . . . the best man . . . he has the groom's ring." My heart beats a thousand times.

"What? Where is he? Explain, explain!" I panic.

"OK, Courtney . . . " She starts off steadily, lowering her hands flat and signaling for me to calm down.

"The boys had their little bachelor party last night and apparently he had too much fun—but don't worry! I'm sure he's just around the hotel. We're gonna find him, sober him up, and he'll be as good as new for the wedding!"

I close my eyes and breathe deeply. In my mind I see a beautiful wedding. Then I tell Alli, "It's OK, it's all right, this is just a minor problem. You're right, he's here, everything is gonna be OK!" I walk away nonchalantly as if I am floating on a cloud. Allison watches as if I'm delusional.

I try to shake the thought of having to slip temporary rings on our fingers. I am so mad at Brian. He's the best man; he should be more responsible than that. I think back to when I first met him and Marcell's other friends. Richard was from school and Raymond used to date one of my friends. Unlike my team, they've known each other most of their lives, since grade school. They share a brotherly love and have stayed by each other's side through all of the events in their lives. They're even open to knowing how each other feels about their girlfriends or wives. I'm close with all of them—they're like big brothers. After we met, the more they approved of me, the more likely I felt that I would become Marcell's wife.

Today, the boys are doing all the handy work for the wedding. I didn't give them any serious responsibilities because, well, they're men.

Besides, I know they're busy keeping Marcell "in check" until the long-awaited moment.

Finally it is time for the last piece to be set in place, my wedding dress. It is a glowing, pearl-white, strapless dress with a flowing train. The veil is long and beautifully lacy and falls over my head to my mid-back. I slip into it thinking I'm all set, but in the back of my mind I know something is missing. I slap my forehead: "Oh my God, I forgot. 'Something old, something new, something borrowed, something blue.' This wedding is going to be a complete disaster!"

The girls shoot each other peculiar looks. Suddenly, Jade hands me the ankle bracelet that I gave her when we were younger. Aris takes a hair clip, baby blue, her favorite color, from her head and pins it in my hair. Melissa and Allison, who love jewelry, present me with a glamorous sparkling diamond earring and necklace set. Last, but certainly not least, my mom walks into the room and gives me my grandmother's garter. "She would have been proud," I say to myself. "She is," my mother whispers, holding both my shoulders from behind. I put everything on delicately and slowly turn towards the long mirror. A tear falls from my eye. "I'm not gonna talk, because I'm gonna drown my makeup!" We share a laugh as we walk out of the room in order.

"They found Brian. He was a little wasted, but the boys cleaned him up and the rings are on the pillow!" Jade whispers in the church hallway. The church's double doors open. The flower girls enter, then the ring bearer, next my girls: Aris, Allison, Jade, then Melissa. When it is my turn, I lock arms with my father. He gives me a look, as if he's proud yet sad to let his little girl go. I lean over to him. "I'm gonna to tell you like everybody's been telling me: Everything is gonna be OK!" I give him a tender kiss on the cheek. From his reaction, I can tell he feels confident now.

When the double doors open, it's as if a breeze of God's grace is shooting through me. Somehow God is willing me to walk, because my knees feel stiff as boards. The first thing I see is the white pathway scattered with lavender rose petals. I match my footsteps to the rhythm of the wedding march, with my father at my left. I feel as if there is a glow around me. As I walk, I inhale the crisp air. With each step I feel I'm farther from my childish and wild ways and closer to a new, fulfilling, and successful life. As I "walk the plank," I glance side to side and am so happy to see everyone I love here, in the flesh, sharing this day of celebration. I realize I couldn't have made it here without them. The church is filled with silver and lavender decorations. The sun is shining so brightly, and I can't help but think that God and my grandmother are watching over me, proud as ever.

I'm closer now, and my heart is beating faster and faster, as if it is about to rip through my dress. I'm a couple of steps away from the altar. The groomsmen are looking more handsome than ever in their black tuxedos with lavender shirts and silver flowers pinned to their lapels. My girls are wearing gorgeous lavender dresses and holding bouquets of silver flowers. The pastor holds an open Bible. Then, finally, the most important sight to behold: I stop right before I hit the altar and glance at my lover. My dad lifts the veil over my face and gives me a gentle kiss and wipes away my teardrop. This is the last thing he can do to make his little girl better. I am now three steps away from the altar.

Step one: Leave my childhood and my last name behind. Step two: No longer single, throw the black book away. Step three: Devote myself and dedicate my life, love, and everything to one man.

At the top step of the altar, I am now side by side with the man I'm going to spend eternity with. I inhale his love and exhale all my worries and stress accepting that God has brought me here today for one reason, and I put my trust in him.

Tears run down his face as he recites his vows. I wipe them away, knowing he truly loves me, watching him set his masculinity aside. I pass my bouquet of flowers to my maid of honor and begin pouring my feelings out to him.

A faint sound could be heard outside our house, but as you entered, it became something totally different.

"Malon, let me in!" I was pounding on the locked door vigorously.

"No, I'm changing," she lied.

"Grrrrr," I growled. My sister always does this when it's time to sleep (we keep all the blankets in her room). This little game raises my stress level, which can be high when you're in high school.

"Malon, stop lying and let me in!" I wasn't about to give up. I saw my mother coming, and I smiled with a sense of victory.

"Malon . . . " I said in a mysterious tone, "Mom's here, so now you have to let me in."

"Stop all this noise! Stop banging on the door!" My mom yelled . . . at . . . me.

"But Mom, Malon won't let me in!"

"Malon, let him in," my mom asked in a sweet voice.

"Mom, I'm changing."

My mother turned to me and pointed to the door. "You see!? She's changing. Now leave her alone!"

She stormed off. I looked at my sister's door and turned to walk away. Before I could take a step, my sister opened the door. She had a sadistic smile on her face. I walked away this time. Mom always takes her side.

I decided to watch TV. My dad was in the living room, opening his letters. All of them were bills. I told him what had happened, and he gave me a serious look.

"Your mother is like that. Get used to it."

I sighed at his words. They sounded blunt and very solemn.

"Look, let me show you something," my father said. He spread out a long piece of paper. I had a puzzled look on my face.

"What is it?" I asked.

"You'll see . . ."

If I had only known, I would have ripped those papers up in an instant . . .

The building started rather small. After my father went through the long and arduous process of getting the permit, our project could finally start. This task was too difficult to accomplish alone, so my father told me he would ask his brothers and my uncle who might be the best men for the job.

His brothers declined, but my uncle said with a smile, "I am." He brought other workers to help us. We began digging. The addition to the house would go over the lawn, so we had to dig through the grass, which can be painful: when you dig up grass, you have to push hard on the ground, which puts up resistance. It hurts your back, and you feel it for a while. It's harder than it looks, but you get used to it.

It was lunchtime, and the workers were eating in the kitchen. I walked into the living room and saw my little brother watching TV.

"Bro, what are you doing in here? Why aren't you helping Dad?" I asked.

"Why aren't you helping him?"

"Because it's lunch and I'm resting."

"Well . . . " My brother thought hard and said, "You're not my mom or dad, so you can't tell me what to do!"

"I'm your older brother. That should be enough!"

Lunch was over and we started to work again. Conversations were cheerful . . . but then, as I was shoveling I accidentally hit my uncle with a piece of dirt. I saw his temper flare and I lowered my head to hide my face.

"Who did that?" he roared. I raised my hand slowly. My uncle came toward me, but my dad stopped him in his tracks. "Back off." My uncle looked at me, then at my dad, and back at me. He shrugged it off and continued working. I was surprised—he had never acted that way before.

It took two weeks, but our digging was complete. I asked if we were ready to build upwards yet. (We could only build the floor at the time.) My father sighed. "Not yet." He went inside the house. Frustrated, I muttered, "This better be worth it."

The next day I asked my dad what the situation was. He showed me the plans, and I looked at them, exasperated. There was so much work to be done!

Another two weeks passed, and it was time to lay the foundation. I was surprised when the truck came and even more surprised that it was still there after my father finished putting in the cement.

"Dad, why is the truck here?"

"There is cement left over."

"So return it."

My dad looked at me and shook his head. "It doesn't work that way. Come on. Start cementing the floor."

As we spread the remaining cement, my uncle came up and said, "Worth every penny, wasn't it?"

"No," my dad shouted. "It wasn't! I paid for cement I didn't need! I lost money because of you!"

"You didn't LOSE money, you used it!"

"That's easy for you to say! It's not your money! If I had gotten the cement piece by piece instead of all at once, I wouldn't have lost so much money!"

"You didn't have to listen to me! No one told you to!"

"You did!"

"Sorry for trying to help!"

As I watched my uncle storm off, I was glad that I stayed out of the argument; I didn't need someone to take out their anger on me. The more I thought about it, whenever my dad yelled at someone, he would take out his anger on me, too. Same with my uncle.

Later that day, when things between my father and my uncle had cooled down, I went to Dad and asked if it was time to build up. He said, "If the inspector OKs it." I was proud. My dad had worked hard.

I missed the inspector's visit, but I was there for the result. It took him a while to show up (a week to be exact), so I was curious when I arrived after school. I walked up to my father, and he said, "It didn't pass."

"What?"

"It was missing something. I'll try to get what it needs." He seemed to be in deep thought. I wanted to ask him what it needed but decided it was best not to ask. I looked around and noticed that even more construction had been done while I was gone. But the building didn't pass.

I came home after school to find my dad installing insulation around the floor. I looked at the insulation and noticed it could cut your hand when you installed it.

"Dad!"

"What!?"

"Are you wearing gloves?!"

"No!"

"Put some on!"

"I'm fine!"

"Put on gloves!"

I continued trying to convince him, but he refused. Besides, he had already finished. I looked at him, then shook my head. Why doesn't he care if his hands get hurt?

The inspector OK'd the building, and I felt good for my dad. This was what he'd been waiting for. We started to build up, but only the floor got finished. As we were working, I noticed that where someone had spilled water on the floor, the wood shriveled a little. "How odd," I thought. Shouldn't wood be able to stand water?

The floor was done and now the infrastructure (it's like a shell) could be built. I watched my dad and the workers from a distance, and I noticed that every once in a while my dad would argue with my uncle. This worried me because it put my dad behind schedule. The other workers would take advantage of the arguing and take a break as long as the arguing lasted. It was as if they accepted the fighting! The building should have been half done by now. I hoped this wouldn't become a routine.

Unfortunately it did become a routine, and it got worse. Each day there was more arguing and less working. We were now a month behind. The shell wasn't completed yet. I wanted them to stop fighting and just work. That wasn't going to happen, though, not for a long time.

I saw the forecast on TV. The reporter said, "The next few days, expect rainy weather." I groaned. Rainy weather was the worst.

The next day seemed like most days. A little argument turned into a big one, and everyone stopped and rested while my dad and my uncle went at it. But this day was different—it was worse than the others. Around 3:30 P.M. the arguing started again, and I couldn't take it anymore. This time I got between them and said:

"Stop! Stop all this fighting! It's not supposed to be like this." I pointed at my uncle. "You! My dad has a limited amount of money and he can't afford to waste a cent." I pointed at my father. "You! You have to understand his point of view . . . "

That's as far as I got. A drop of rain fell on my head. I looked up. "Oh no. . . " The wood was getting wet from the rain, and it wasn't a little dribble—it was a downpour.

We all went inside, and I watched as the project started to collapse under the rain. I turned around and said, "Dad, you can still do this, right?" He said there was no money left for the room. I looked at my dad and my uncle, and I yelled, "Are you happy?! The rain is ruining my future bedroom, and it's all your fault. Could you not compromise!? Could you not work together?! If you were the father and uncle I know and not the arguers that are here, then my room would have been done! Do you know how rough it is to sleep on a couch instead of a bed?"

I turned around and looked at the ruined heap. It would have been nice to have a room built with teamwork, but my uncle and my dad's arguments made sure that would never be.

A SHORT BROWN MAN
ASHLEY GRUBBS

The phone rang three times before my father answered. I had to find out what time he would be coming by to get us. It was a hot summer morning filled with the sweet smell of bacon and Sugar Smacks. The sound of Lucky barking at the wind began making me mad. When my dad finally picked up, I yelled:

"Hey Daddy. Happy Father's Day!"

"Hey Baby. Thank you very much." He was quiet for a second. "Baby, do me a big favor?"

"Anything."

"Put your momma on the phone," he said in a downhearted manner.

I gave my mother the phone and went back to watching Nick Jr. on TV. The phone hit the floor. I jumped and sat there helplessly as my mother cried. My first thought was to call my sister Traci. Traci is older than me and would know what to do.

"Traci, Mommy is crying," I yelled. Traci entered the living room along with our grandparents, whose house we were visiting. She was wearing one of the "good" dresses that my father had bought her. The pink dress stood out: it was a long dress with a pink bow. Her hair was in three pigtails, with pink and white hair balls. She hated this dress, but our father loved her in it. My mother made her wear it every time we went somewhere nice with him.

"Momma, what's the matter?" asked Traci. She sat by my mom on the arm of the sofa. I could see that she was going to cry, too.

"Baby, pick up the phone and talk to your father," my mother said. Traci picked up the phone.

"Daddy?" she questioned. The phone hit the floor once again. Traci ran up the stairs and closed herself in our room.

I stood there completely lost. I knew something wasn't right, but what? I looked at my mother and tried to fight back tears; but I couldn't control myself anymore. I stood in the middle of the living room in my yellow dress, the dress with little white flowers on it and a white bow that came around my body and tied in the back. Being the tomboy that I was, I hated wearing anything that was pretty.

My grandmother hurried back into the kitchen to take the bacon out of the pan. I walked slowly over to my mother, my head hung low.

"Baby, your father is coming over so that he can talk to you."

"About what, Mommy?"

"He'll tell you when he gets here."

Finally, he arrived. I jumped up and ran to him. I could see that he had been crying.

"Daddy, what's the matter?"

"Come here and sit on my lap. I need to talk to you about somethin'."

"OK." I sat on his lap and studied his face. He looked sleepy.

"So what's the matter with ya'll? Why is everyone crying?" I asked.

"Well, I really don't know how to say this—"

"Just say it then."

"Paw-paw died today."

"What? You're lying to me! That's not funny! He can't be dead! He promised that he would always be there for me."

I tried to fight my way out of my father's arms.

"Let go of me! I don't believe you."

I fell down to the ground and started to cry. He picked me up and held on to me. I continued to struggle. He pulled me close to his chest and started to cry. Even though I tried to get out of his arms, he continued to comfort me.

June 15, 1991, was the day he was called home. He was a short, brown-skinned man with a "Homie the Clown" haircut. He wore glasses, like most of his children. His fat face did not reveal his age: he looked thirty but was really sixty-five. For many years he coached football at Washington High School in South Central Los Angeles. He became famous on the street for his coaching ability. He wanted to be the best at everything that he did. He always used to say, "We must work as a team. We must work for a common goal, so that we can succeed." As he slept, early that Father's Day morning, his soul left his body, only to join the others that had left before him. Just two days earlier, he was out in the back yard playing with my sister and me around the cherry and lemon trees that he had planted for us. Just the night before, he was telling us that he would always be there for us.

After the death of my grandfather, things moved slowly for me. It seemed like life was passing me by. It felt as if there was a weight holding me back. I found myself trying to run, but couldn't. I wanted to die. He was gone and I wanted to be with him; I just wanted to be with him. I knew that my family needed me, but what was I to do? My best friend was gone. My whole world was gone. With his death, I felt as if someone had betrayed me and my family. I wanted to find the person responsible for letting him go and introduce them to my pain. Deep down inside, I felt hate. I wanted revenge.

But by hating that person, I was not helping my team—I was only hurting it. What my family needed was to stick together. You see, the team was no longer working for a common goal. The goal was to bring the family back together, to stop the fighting, but there seemed to be only one person who could bring the team back together, and he was gone.

Even though my grandfather was gone, the family eventually learned to stick together. We just needed to work a little harder. And over time, we realized: We had been looking at his death as a bad thing, but it was a good thing. He was now free.

To end my strife
I'm gonna commit poetic suicide.
I slice my pen in half and watch as it bleeds
Staining the paper in the form of verse . . .

So the ink and paper start to converse,
Creating my definition of poetry and life.
United like husband and wife, husband and wife,
Husband and wife.
Prone to break apart but destined to reunite . . .

Destined to reunite like my pen and my knife . . .
All I need is one more slice to get my mind to the point of the next line.
So the husband offers his future wife a symbol of love, trust, and
Commitment, and she gives in.
So the pen offers his ink and the paper, she gives in,
Creating the verse that your eyes now digest.
Feeding your souls with the woes of my contemplation,
Without hesitation I express my frustration . . .

Husband and wife
Wife and husband
Paper and pen
Pen and paper
Ink and metaphors
Metaphors and ink

Let me convert this into something that will reach its arms out and
kidnap the minds of the poetic nation.
Sending them into a trance.
Making them weak and vulnerable to my thoughts,

So I drown them in depth.

I drown so deep *so deep . . . so deep . . . so deep*

So when they reach the surface they see what I see. Feel what I feel when I see my fellow brothas and sistahs die. They see why I cry. Why I'm frustrated when everyone else is caught up, better yet, wrapped up, in their materialistic ways.

We have the children being bought and sold to make your
Fancy designer clothes.
But forgive me for I have forgotten that's not part of the story that you have been told.
Let me unfold the secrets that will threaten the minds of the young and old.
How many of you know of the mothers in Cambodia who sell their children for fifteen dollars?
How many of you hear the silent cries of Mother Africa as we sit back and Watch as her breed dies?
We are suffocating under our hazy skies, we can't hear the silent but oh- so-violent cries of the Motherland.
They are not cries for civilization; they are cries of agony, pain, and strife.

I say we march hand in hand into the sunrise and let our eyes be exposed to the sunlight,
Helping those with distorted vision,
Because it seems that Clear Eyes and Visine still aren't
Helping people see what needs to be seen.
It seems we're too busy blinding others, we can't see ourselves clearly.
And if we can't see ourselves clearly, then we grow weary and fade into the background and our voices make no sound.
They jus' fade until we become a majority, and that majority becomes a minority, and that minority becomes something that people generalize and fail to realize that we're still here.
And in fear they label us and smother us until we are no longer seen.
So we have to work as a team to break down the barrier of "superiority"
And let our voices be fed to the ears that deny their hunger and the knowledge we hold.

A GARDEN OF ROSES
SANDRA GONZALEZ

A loving family is like a garden of roses that never stops growing.

Roses depend on soil like children depend on parents.

Soil nurtures roses the way family members nurture each other.

Water gives life to roses the way patience and support create family unity.

Sunlight gives life to roses the way parents give love to their kids.

It was 12:30 A.M., and the light was on. I woke up, confused. The paramedics had come to take my little sister. I heard my family members sobbing and the soft pounding of footsteps. The saintly sounds of the paramedics ascending the stairs made me dizzy. As I cleared my thoughts, I heard my panic-stricken mother saying that my sister was unconscious. She needed oxygen and couldn't get it.

I hadn't realized there was a family secret. My mother confessed that when my sister was four years old, she had been diagnosed with epilepsy and mental retardation. The doctors told my mother that she would have seizures, many of them, one after another. As years passed, she did in fact have numerous seizures that lasted for two to three minutes each.

But this seizure was different. This time, they didn't stop coming; they came one after another. And my mother didn't know what to do. An hour later, she picked up the phone and dialed 911. Minutes passed, but it seemed like an eternity before the ambulance arrived.

For the next few days we felt powerless. We didn't know if my sister was going to survive or not. We spent the longest days of our lives running back and forth between home and the hospital. Finally, my sister opened her eyes. With the help of her doctors, she was like a newborn. Her eyes opened as if to say, "I'm alive." Her recovery wasn't just due to great doctors—a united family inspired her to keep fighting. She deserved a second chance.

As I reflect on this experience, I realize it would have been easy for us to give up and get lost in our hopelessness, but my family stuck together. Love, care, patience, and understanding came into play. We had to support each other. My sister needed all of our attention; we had to step it up as a family and forget about the boundaries we had built between us over the years.

As I was growing up, my parents and I didn't communicate with each other much. Most of the time my parents gave their full attention to my sister instead of me. I often felt uncomfortable talking to my parents, as if I was a stranger. We eventually broke down the walls that had separated us over time and "rediagnosed" the meaning of family.

MY FAMILY

NOEL MUÑOZ

Waking up every morning wanting to help my mother
Going to school and trying to make it because I love her
I'm trying not to worry about me,
The people I put first are my family
I'm the big bro, but I feel sometimes like the parent
I always want to control my siblings, I think it's genetic
I'm trying to stop Brenda, fifteen years old, from making a mistake
She's always outside, I feel like her life is at stake
Gangstas always shooting, not caring who they hit
I tell her to watch out so she'll never meet a bullet
Maribel, thirteen years old, has been acting kind of funny,
She never helps me clean, she doesn't care if our house smells funky
She thinks going to school is her only job
I tell her to help me and stop being lazy and she begins to sob
My only little brother, Gerardo, eleven years old, is trying to be like me,
We were a good combination like Shaq and Kobe
Back in the day he would never talk back
Now he thinks he's all that
But for the last couple of months we've been having issues,
I fight with him about little things like picking up his shoes
The youngest in my family, Rocio, nine years old, has to be the worst;
She's always yelling, screaming, and loves to curse.
I try to stop her from acting bad
She's always acting like that. It makes my mom sad.

My family had never really experienced death
But last year my grandma was in bad health
When she died, my dad lost it
When we went to the hospital he would try to avoid it

I remember all of us trying to get him to go
He would be on the couch watching some show
My sisters, brother, and I begged him to come with us
But he would just make an excuse and fuss
Until finally he decided it was time
When we went a lot of people were there crying
It was a bad time for us, seeing someone we loved dying
This is the first time we had really come together as a family
When we were there none of us were looking happy
Every other day we would all go to the hospital
We would pray to get her out of there as soon as possible
But when she died we weren't there, it was a Saturday night
My family felt sad but we knew she went to a better place
When she died we tried to act like one team
But the feelings we had were like from a bad dream.

After this experience there was a new connection with me and my family
I found out they will always be there for me
So when my parents tell me not to do something I know why
They want me to live a full life and don't want me to die
When other families are having issues with their kids banging
I try to study while my neighbors are slanging
My parents just want what's best for me
I struggle to become the person they want me to be
Both parents work hard day and night
They taught me that doing drugs is bad and going to school is right
My family sticks together, although we fight
This family of mine will always be tight.

WE ARE FRIENDS, WE WERE ENEMIES
VALERIE CORRAL

It all started in the sixth grade. It was Monday when a new girl, Amy, came to school. It was refreshing to have someone new join my elementary school. She looked loyal, smart, and the type who stays out of trouble, so I introduced myself to her, knowing that she didn't have any friends. I asked if she would like to hang out with me and my friends. She said yes. It was so exciting to have a new member of the crowd. I already had a best friend, Ariel, but that was soon going to change.

The boys all wanted to go out with Amy, but she would say, "No," or "You don't even know me." All the girls in school didn't like her, but they didn't even try to get to know her. We became so close; I forgot that I already had a best friend. We became the new best friends in school. When Ariel noticed what was happening, she suddenly started to ignore me. That was a surprise to me. I didn't know what I was doing. I just thought, "Oh, maybe I did something wrong."

I got to know Amy, but I didn't see how bad she really was or how many problems she had. Her parents were always fighting, and they were on the edge of getting a divorce. They would always choose Amy's brother over her all of the time. They would always blame Amy for the evil things her little brother would do, like break crystals in the house. She was also doing drugs.

When I found out she was doing drugs, I was extremely shocked and disappointed in her. I felt worried for Amy and myself. I was disappointed in myself for getting dragged into this mess, and I was also worried about disappointing my family. In my family, the best side to be on is the good side. If my family were to know about this, what would they think of me? Would they say what they always say: "There's no way to change her, she's turned upside down." They would just give up on me and not even consider a second chance. Sad, right?

One time during PE, Amy brought cigarettes and a lighter; we were not allowed to have those things on campus, but she brought them. We went to this place where all the cool kids hang around. There is a fence, and people pass through and check us out. We attracted the whole class around us, including Ariel, making it a lot easier to get caught. But who cares? I thought we looked cool. Then my sixth-grade teacher, Mr. Brown, had to ruin all the fun and tell us to move from the spot. Everyone left, including Ariel, who walked to the swing set. She wanted me to go with her. I didn't want to go, so I said with attitude, "No." Ariel had been ignoring me all semester, and I just didn't feel like going with her. Then the teacher noticed that Amy and I didn't move. He noticed something suspicious was going on, and he asked, "What are you kids doing?" We replied, "We're just kicking it." He said, "Well, just kick it somewhere else." Did we listen? No. We stayed right where we were. We defied Mr. Brown's orders and got into trouble. I wish I would've gone with Ariel.

I learned that getting into trouble isn't always the cool thing to do. It is important to choose the right friends and not leave the good ones behind. I also learned that I will have to stay away from disappointment, my biggest fear, and not hold in my emotions all the time.

Now comes the big question: Should I tell mom?

I kept this from my mom for about a month, but my conscience was killing me every day. My stomach hurt so badly, like a volcano had erupted. One day my mom and I were alone in the house. I heard my mom in my little brother's room. That was my big chance to tell her, and I took it. I let it all out and told my mother what stupidity I had gotten myself into. I told her not to be mad at anyone else but me. Her facial expressions said more than words could explain—she was so disappointed. I burst into tears. I had never gotten into trouble. I felt like I had landed in a hole.

The only thing I could think about was what type of example I may have set for my little brothers. My family has a history of turning away the screwups of the family. Will they disown me, too, and kick me off their team? Will I ever gain back my mom's trust? Had I disappointed my family? What will people think of me? What will happen now? What? What! I had let down my team. Even as I hid in self-pity, the person I really felt sorry for was Amy. She had no one to talk to.

I bet she didn't even tell her parents. Her parents were kind of abusive. Who knows what her parents would have done to her? She would never say that, but no one believed her. Come on, bruises? She would say she was play-fighting with her parents. Anytime she would try to impress them, they would always throw any little bad thing in her face, like the type of friends she hung out with or the time she spent on the street. She probably felt like she wasn't good enough. That must suck!

After I told my mom, we talked about how I felt in this situation. She thought it was OK to tell Amy's mom, but I wasn't OK with my mom snitching. I told her how good I felt to let it all out myself. Then I asked her a question: "Don't you think that Amy should have that chance too?" Somehow that convinced her, because I kept my mom from blurting everything out to Amy's mom.

It was time to go back to hell—school! When I went back to school both Amy and Ariel were ignoring me. I found out that somehow Amy knew of my mom's dirty little plan to tell her secrets, or maybe she just felt it coming. Rumors flew around the school about how she wanted to fight me. I wasn't scared, but I was worried. How did she find out? It's funny, but scary. Best friends one day, enemies the next.

Amy finally came up to me and said, "I know you told your mom. If my mom finds out about any of this, I will kick your butt!!!" Then she hit me right on the jaw!

I said, "Damn, you didn't need to hit me; she isn't gonna blab." Then I said, "I think you should tell your mom about what we did." She left with a look of anger and disappointment. I think she knew that telling someone else instead of keeping it all inside would be for the better. I left feeling relieved; at least I told her how I felt. After all the mess, somehow her attitude changed. Maybe she felt sorry about hitting me. Maybe she explained her story to someone else. Who knows? All I know is that she had a lot of things to figure out by herself. I just wish I could've helped a lot sooner.

A year passed, and I felt that Amy was no longer mad about the sixth-grade incident. It was the start of eighth grade, and I knew she was still involved in trouble. But I also knew that I wasn't going to follow my family's pattern and leave her upside down. I knew there was something I could do.

One day during fourth period, Amy sat next to me and passed me a note. We both knew that passing a note in class was an easy way to get in trouble, but I thought this was important. I wasn't going to risk not being able to help her this time. I know it is important to have someone there for you. It started out with a joke about what stupidity we had gotten involved in; then she wrote questions that only a friend would ask. That's how I knew that she wanted a friend, or at least someone to talk to. Class was over and we ended up hanging out for the rest of the day and most of the year.

I did stay close friends with Amy, and she didn't do the things that she did before. As for not listening and getting into trouble, she cleaned up her life a bit. We became a team and we discussed the problems we'd had in the past. And Ariel and I stayed friends, too. The only negative thing is that the friends Ariel chose weren't the best people to hang around with. They didn't like me very much, and I didn't like them. They were conceited, and all they did was talk about people. No one liked them, so it wasn't just me.

Ariel, Amy, her friends, my friends, our friends. The one lifelong lesson I've learned is that there are all types of friends. You can be best friends one day, enemies the next. What really matters is that you have someone there for you.

THE HARD MAKES IT THE GREAT
RANDY PALACIOS

Up at 8:30 A.M., I run and smell the fresh morning air and feel the cool wind. If I trip, I know one of my brothers will ask, "Palacios, you OK?" and I would answer, "Yeah," and he would lift me up. Doing push- ups, seeing the suffering and sweat and tears of coming together—this was hard, but *the hard makes it the great.*

We leave no one behind as we run to get to Sentinel field, running a mile in under eight minutes. Those who don't make it have to run again. Doing crunches about fifty times in sets of thirty, running up and down the bleachers 'til we trip over at least one—I see in hindsight our bond at that moment in time. There were times when we sat in study hall to be sure everyone had the grades to play. There were times we helped each other in subjects such as Spanish, math, and history. We prepared each other for upcoming exams. This was Ánimo Inglewood's Eagles J.V. and varsity basketball team. This was teamwork at its best. Or was it?

Unfortunately, we really didn't come together as a team because everyone wasn't eligible to play. We didn't make enough time to help each other with grades because half of us were thinking about ourselves. For our selfishness, half of my brothers were cut from the family.

To win, sometimes team members need to help their teammates with their personal lives and be there for them when they need it, to try to make sure they have everything going smoothly in their lives before stepping on the court. Coming together is a beginning, keeping it together is progress, and working together is success.

We completed the first step in coming together, but keeping it together didn't happen. Basketball requires cooperation, understanding, and interacting with others. No individual can put himself above the team. If we would have accomplished this we would have had a more successful season, maybe a winning streak.

Instead, we had to get new players during the middle of the season because so many students were ineligible; we had to start back at step one. Having to gain the trust of new players in such a short amount of time was difficult; when they were put on the team, we had four days before our next game. It turned out to be impossible, because it takes a huge amount of time to really trust someone. The results: we didn't win a single game for the rest of the season.

Another reason we didn't come together was that many players wanted to be superstars. You have to sacrifice all that for the team. Alone you can score thirty points a game, but if you lose, it's pointless. The reason you score is to win as a team, not to win for yourself just because you think you are a first-rate baller. That's not teamwork.

You get a win by giving assists and making sure that almost everyone touches the ball. Not only do *they* shine, *you* shine, just like "The Legend," Larry Bird was a sweet shooter who became famous because he worked as a team player and did anything to help his team win.

All of this effects our next season because now everyone has to realize that, as Phil Jackson said, "To make a great team everyone has to sacrifice the me for the we." Teamwork is a chain, and everyone is a link. The chain will weaken if there is a selfish person—just look at the Lakers during the 2004–05 season.

Without teamwork, we Eagles might end up like the Lakers. It's going to be a struggle, and we'll have to learn to trust each other. On the court, you are not going to give the ball to a person whom you don't trust to score, or to someone who may have the ball taken from him. You would rather take the ball in on your own.

The way you can make trust happen between your teammates is to take the time to really get to know them. Getting to know a person means putting everything aside and listening to what they have to say about family or school or just about anything. A team must put all egos aside. For the Eagles, this is going to be a difficult task to accomplish, but as I said before, *the hard makes it the great.*

MUSIK 'N' ME
ISHMAEL NAYLOR

I was first exposed to music at seven or eight, when I was hangin' out with my big homies, my brother-in-law Seneca and his homeboys Wayne and Herm. That night we went to the Inglewood versus Morningside basketball game. I don't remember who won, but it hardly matters now. Afterwards we went out to eat, and we got some pizza, hot wings, and watched the Lakers game.

As we were driving around, Herm was like, "I got this CD by Nas."

"Which one?" Seneca asked.

"I got that *Illmatic*."

So he popped that in and they were talkin' about Nas's style and whatnot. They were sayin' stuff like, "His flows are tight!" and "Nas is one of the realest MCs out."

But Seneca was like, "Nah, you crazy, it's all about Pac."

So he took out *Illmatic* after the last track went off and popped in Tupac's *Me Against the World*. I don't remember what song was playing, but I've been a Tupac and Nas fan ever since.

After hearing those CDs, it was all over. I just had to find out more about hip-hop and music, period. I took my older sister's CD case and listened to damn near every CD in there. NWA, Nas, Tupac, Public Enemy, Westside Connection, Xzibit, everybody—I fell asleep with earphones on that night.

From the beginning, hip-hop just drew me in. It was the feeling behind the lyrics, like what the artist was tryin' to say. Sure, I love the beat and the excitement. Some songs call out to me and it's like I can listen to that one song all day, every day, and not get tired of it. I can still be as hyped the fiftieth time I've listened to it as I was the first time I heard it. I still can't help but nod my head to the beat with a big grin on my face. It just pulls me in, and unless an adult tells me, "No, you can't listen to music," I will always have my earphones with me.

Back in the day, when I was about thirteen, I wrote lyrics just for fun—nothing too serious. Then one day I let my cousin Stephan read what I had written. After he was done, he said, "These are tight. You ever thought of makin' a demo or anything?"

I replied, "Nah, that sounds like lots of fun, but I wouldn't even know where to start."

He helped me write and let me watch him in his creative process and see how he does it, and my level of writing has continued to develop ever since. Workin' with my cousin, I started carrying a pen with me, so when ideas pop up, I can write them down. I started doing this on a piece of paper, on my arms, wherever, so I can look at it later and get to work.

These days, when I'm just kickin' it, someone will put on an instrumental and someone (most of the time, me) will say, "Bust it, bust it." We'll go in a circle freestylin', and everyone will pick up where the last dude left off. We'll spit a few bars, and by the time it's my turn, I know what I'm gonna start off sayin' and where I want my flow to go. But since I'm so silly I just break out laughin'. Everyone knows it's gonna happen every time, so I think I'm getting set up sometimes; I still try.

My homies know me and how much I love music. They feel the same way, so they'll say, "Try doin' this, and this," 'til I build up my skills as a freestyler. You know, they're pulling together as a team to help me out, help me develop as an artist and lyricist. My friends are a big influence on me and my music because I kept my rhymes and freestyles to myself until they encouraged me to put my stuff out there for people to hear. Once I can find my own voice, I'll be able to spit some ill stuff and I will be more open to sharin' my lyrics with people. Because if I'm going to do it, I don't want to go out there and sound like 50 Cent or Jay-Z or whomever. (They are some of my favorite artists, don't get me wrong, but I need to cultivate my own voice.) So if I'm going to be an MC, I just gotta find out my own personal lyrical style and just be me. My friends do their best to help me out, and I have nothing but respect for what they have to say.

Sometimes, though, it's better to just sit down by myself and work. When I'm alone, I'm focused, and I'm all about getting down to business. The energy is different too. Like when I'm just in my room tryin' to freestyle to a beat, I'm just talkin' like I would normally talk to anyone—not too loud and not too quiet. But when I'm with the homies and I'm all hyped, I just let it all go. I just rap my lyrics, loud and full of feelin' and energy, as if I was in a studio layin' down a track. I love every moment of it, but I would rather be alone most of the time, so I don't have any outside interference messing with my train of thought.

My personal opinion on hip-hop (without sounding too cliched), is that you have to have respect for the old-school artists like Run DMC, Naughty By Nature, Public Enemy, Dr. Dre, Pac, and Notorious B.I.G. (just to name a few, 'cause the list goes on and on). You don't have to like their music or their style, but if you wanna get into the game, you gotta recognize the people who came before you, because they created and still dominate the game. They are where you are trying to be, so respect should be there automatically. 'Cause after that night in the car, even at the age of seven, I wanted to study up on the people who came before me. They represent the level I want to reach with my music.

Whatever you do in life, there is always goin' to be someone or something that's gonna make you want to reach that next level. It's the same for musik 'n' me. All these new artists are tight, so that makes me want to up my game so I can actually compete with them, instead of ending up as a one-hit wonder. Once you have found that thing or that person that pushes you, draw from it, and you'll be surprised what you can achieve. PEACE!

THE KISS
ARLYN JIMENEZ

I waited three long years for this beloved moment to come
The day he had me feeling as wild and vibrant as a cherry plum

We were in the light of the night's dark stars, the loving connection
of he and I
When my seductive lips and his finally united, we could not deny

He was like the rose's smooth petals as they open and began to shed
And I was as strong as the thorny stem, he said

We weren't just petals and stem, but an enchanting alluring rose
Our appealing scent brought us together, wherever the wind would blow

There is no I or you in the passionate love we both shared
We worked together to solve our problems because we both cared

At night I now hear my lonely tears searching for his deep eternal love
Love: a confusing puzzle that only two hearts can solve

I never thought this lovable creature would fall into my arms
I looked at his lovely smile and basked in all his charms

It takes two devoted hearts to make one affectionate kiss last
It takes courage to hold the puzzle together to see real love amassed

Act I, Scene I

NOT FAR FROM A GIRL SCOUT CAMP

A butterfly flutters by and catches the eye of an innocent, curious, unsuspecting little Girl Scout. She becomes entranced by that fluttering butterfly and is lured through the forest. Unaware of how far out she is going, she gets caught up in the grasp of freedom. Cookies in hand, adorned in sash and badges recognizing the numerous tasks she has accomplished, the little girl walks along pulling her red wagon. Seven years on this earth, she tumbles into a hidden ditch.

Caught beneath a mass of tendrils, she struggles to get free. Tiny waterfalls trickle down her face. She realizes that she is just beside a tree. She stops for a moment to take it all in. It seems so vast to her inexperienced eyes. She clutches herself with her arms. The immensity of the forest almost overwhelms her in its might. The world seems so intimidating, as if at any moment it will engulf her.

High in the tree above . . . a nest! High in its boughs lay this particular bird nest. It belongs to none other than Shirley and George Sparrow.

George, your typical male archetype, is sitting in his lazy bird chair, while Shirley, your caring housewife type, is looking outside the nest when all of the commotion began with the little Girl Scout.

SHIRLEY
That poor girl, if only she could've flown. Falling on her head like that will leave a nasty mark. There's nobody there left to help her, George! She's so young and inexperienced still. I bet nobody even knows where she is.

The little girl begins to cry when she sees that some flowers were crushed when she fell. George is still sitting, reading the Daily Cardinal *in his lazy bird chair . . . still ignoring his wife.*

SHIRLEY
How can you not feel sympathy for that girl?

GEORGE
Shirley, leave that to them . . . we can take care of our own.

SHIRLEY
You know, we should go down and sit with her. You didn't say anything when those nice Girl Scouts nursed your wing back to health last fall. I was so embarrassed after you came trotting in here and fell out of the tree. Remember, George, you and those crows (*sighs*) . . . they always get you into trouble. They say they are going to take you out for casual drinking . . . but you come in here like some cat strung on that nip! You should know better by now, George!

GEORGE
You leave me be. Shirley, you're always squawking around here like some hen! Just to show what you know, I haven't had a drink of nectar since!

SHIRLEY
(*Sarcastically*) Well, dear, I'm so proud of you. You've realized you do have self-control. Now back to the girl, George. Just look at her. She is down there crying her little eyes out.

The little girl is wailing uncontrollably.

SHIRLEY
She just wandered out here in the forest all by her lonesome after she followed that butterfly around. There was a big thud and the crushing of the vines as she fell into the ditch. Oh, you should have seen it, George! I hate to see another soul in such pain. This is so awful. It's just terrible, George.

GEORGE
I'm not listening to this. You're going crazy! You don't have to worry about me; I'm not going to pull my feathers out worrying about some know-nothing human who can't even walk without getting themselves caught in some ditch! It's a nice day out, Shirley, fresh air, clear blue skies, the neighbors are out singing . . . go join them!

The little girl hears the loud chirping of the birds above her and stops crying. She wonders how she can help them calm down.

GEORGE
You have to let these things play out by themselves . . . I've been around the block a few times, Shirley. I know a thing or two about human affairs. Humans are incapable of handling their own dilemmas . . . and believe you me, they have a lot of them! The times have changed, Shirley . . . you've got to let these things go. When humans even come within a mile of each other, chaos reigns heavily over them. They are incapable of solving any discrepancies they might have, darling.

SHIRLEY
Huh George? You say something? Well, that's wonderful, dear. But how can you just sit there at a time like this? Look, her forehead is swollen and red. She's getting up, George! Oh, it looks like it's so painful. The soreness, aching, throbbing, oh I just can't imagine! Looks like she's got something in her mouth . . . like grass. What a horrid taste.

GEORGE
(Impatiently) Shirley, for the last time . . .

All of a sudden the sound of boots starts to materialize in the silence of the forest. Girl Scouts run up in a frenzy. They rally together to rescue their youngest seedling! They set up an express, do-it-yourself triage of sorts on the forest floor. The little woodland creatures scurry all around in the hustle and bustle of the triage area. Gurney and first-aid kits are passed down a line. You can just see the relief spread across the little girl's face. One of the Girl Scouts suspects that their little sprout has a broken arm. They scramble to put her arm in a splint decorated with butterflies. Now they pack up and go marching off into the distance. She'll never forget this experience!

SHIRLEY
Oh, finally someone has come out to get her . . . I feel a little bit better now. *(Sarcastically)* I guess you were right about the complications of human affairs, because they are incapable of getting by in life without the help of George Tobias Sparrow, huh dear?! Well, guess what, George . . . they can get by without you just satisfactory!

GEORGE
Don't patronize me, Shirley . . .

SHIRLEY
Just let me know when you are going to make another generalization about humans, George . . . that way I can go get something to plug my ears!

GEORGE
(Glaring at Shirley) Hmm! Well, I guess they can get along without killing each other in the process. But you just wait, Shirley . . . it's not like she's going to stay sweet and innocent for the rest of her cursed life here on this wretched little human-infested world!

SHIRLEY
(Sternly) George, what has gotten into you? I will not accept the fact that you have turned into an evil, maniacal, prude male! *(Sarcastically)* I mean you have to give them some credit . . . they can't all be as sharp as you!

GEORGE
(Looks back down at his paper) That's right, dear . . . I'm glad you've finally figured that out. Now will you please just come and sit down. Have some of the birdseed they left for us.

SHIRLEY
Oh! George, honestly . . . how can you be so bitter and inconsiderate?!

GEORGE
Well, Shirley . . . when I see your lovely face each morning, it makes me forget I even have a care in the world!

SHIRLEY
Oh, George!

(Birds peck)

THE END

There I was again, getting dropped off at the same airport. Seeing people I may have known but didn't recognize. Not as nervous as the year before, looking forward to having fun. Looking forward to seeing Jess and Em. Not realizing that I would find myself this summer and that these unfamiliar faces would soon become ones I would never forget. They would become etched in my mind together with hurt and joy. Again, I'd made it to Camp Heartland.

It wasn't just an ordinary camp. It was a week-long summer getaway designed to accommodate kids "affected or effected" by the HIV/AIDS virus; it was an outlet for those who tortured themselves or were teased for loving someone who had this disease or had the virus themselves. OK, let me backtrack . . .

My first year, as I prepared for camp, I was completely lost. Other than being overly confident (which some consider to be a disease!), I was completely healthy. Then I learned that in order to attend this camp I had to be connected with the HIV virus in some way. Next came the conversation where she relieved herself of this information, dropped this load onto my shoulders, a secret that I wouldn't be able to share. The eye contact I denied her, the lack of emotion in her voice. It's funny how you can be so blind to the obvious: all of the medicine she had been taking, all the restrictions in the shelter we were living in, all the bulletins and flyers associated with the virus. I should have known something was wrong with my mother.

Closeness—when you *really* know a person—can separate you from logic. Just when you think you understand something, it turns out to be something else. It came as a shock to me that my mom was positive, but I shrugged it off, content, or so I thought.

That first year of camp was fun, but it wasn't exactly the comfort zone, a place to forget, that it was to others. Not that year.

My second year at camp seemed pretty much the same at first, but it turned out to be totally different. I'd been living openly with my mother and her illness for a year but was unable to tell anyone, not knowing if simply being her teenage child might hurt her. Looking back, if it wasn't for Shai, Stacy, and all the others with me on the Adventure Program (A.P.) at Camp Heartland that year—those who have been through so much more than I could ever handle—I would never have realized how blessed I was.

Camp! When I first arrived that second year, I almost felt free. It was the most calming environment I'd ever been in. The smell of fresh air, the light warm breeze, the ocean-blue sky. The warm embraces I received as soon as I got off the bus: There was love and energy there. There was reassurance. There were open ears. Jess was there! Jessica Brumm, my open arms, my confidant, my ears, my heart. With her as my journal, my speak into, I found myself. Camp found me. Camp had finally become, for me, what it was for everyone else: my comfort zone.

Even though I was in the program for kids ages fourteen to fifteen again, I still had different counselors, a different group of kids, different activities. At that point, I didn't know how much I would learn from— and grow attached to—them.

In A.P., our adventures went beyond the physical. We were open to everyone else's life adventures, whether they were exciting, scary, or even dangerous. In sharing these adventures, we established trust; by the end of this week, we would bond. Many things took place in this short time span—and it turned out to be life-changing for me. We had group talks and group strengthening activities. We really dug into the issue of HIV/AIDS and our connection to it.

It still amazes me how certain circumstances can motivate you. All the stories I heard seemed so much worse than my own! From one side of the room I heard: "I was born with the AIDS virus." From another side: "My mother was addicted to drugs so I was born addicted to crack." From the back of the room: "My father is in the last stages of his life, but he's strong, and now I feel like he's my motivation to stay strong." Hearing all this, I thanked God that my case was not as bad and asked him to show me if my future might contain similar pain. That was the day that started it all, the day when I no longer just sympathized with them, but *became* them. That was the group discussion that triggered something in my mind, saying: This is why you're here.

It was a domino effect, from the sex talks about how to protect ourselves from getting the virus or passing it on, to the night on the beach. Every year the A.P. spent a night off-site and since we were in Malibu, we spent the night on the beach. We put up three tents: one for the girls, one for the boys, and one for the counselors. We made chuck wagons for dinner, took turns cutting up different vegetables, put together an assembly line to wrap the chuck wagons and cook them. That night we even had s'mores—it was a complete camping experience! Later, right before we all went to sleep, we passed around this little bag of cards with different words on them, such as "wisdom," "power," "love." We called them the "Angel Cards," and we each told of a person, event, or whatever we thought the word meant to us and why. It may seem like just a common game, something you can do anywhere, but it was more. It helped me to figure out who and what had influenced me. It helped me figure out who I was. That night felt so true, so safe, so right. Learning how to connect with others, filling their empty spaces and finding that they contain the piece you're missing. Working together to feel better, to complete each other, to hold each other up when we feel like tearing ourselves down. That's what camp became for me, that's what the people there gave me. They gave me myself, what I could no longer hide from the world. They were my team, my group, my support system.

Leaving camp that year was extremely hard for me. I had to leave my bed of comfort and go back to the heartaching reality that was my life. So many tears shed! Looking back, maybe they saw how I had changed, even though it took me months to figure it out myself. After a while, I just sucked it up and told myself, "You'll be back next year."

With the confidence and reassurance I received at camp, it was time for me to go home and address this life of mine face to face instead of hiding behind my hurt, my fear, and my doubt! Using the life skills I received from my new team, I came home, and instead of simply living with my mother physically, I lived with her emotionally and mentally. Through open conversations about her health and the stress of daily life, I understood her pain and her fears—and together, we now face life each day with God as our guide. We became a team, clearing all doubts, facing all fears, and healing all pain with knowledge and unconditional love.

MY SOLDIERS
GABRIEL GAMEZ

My soldiers
They're right by my side
They never leave me alone
In bad times
When we get shot at
Or jacked for our cheddar

And in good times
When we hang out and play football
No matter what, they will be there
On that rocky road
Of bull**** and lies
We will fight this battle
To get through the journey
To survive in the hood

And this is winning, surviving
And it will be paradise and heaven
And it's home sweet home
Because we accomplish the thing we want most . . .
Happiness

My soldiers put their lives on the line
Hand by hand we march on
And we die for one another
Because we love each other like brothers
And this is the unspoken love of soldiers.

So I thank you, my soldiers.

SCREENPLAY

FADE IN:
EXT. STREET CORNER,
COMPTON – DAY

MARCUS, a fifteen-year-old African American, sees a beautiful young WOMAN waiting at the BUS STOP:

>MARCUS
>A, Monica! Hold up!

>MONICA
>Oh, hey Marc.

>MARCUS
>Since when do you take the bus?

>MONICA
>My mom changed her hours so now she can't drop me off.

>MARCUS
>Serious? A, don't take the bus home. Those dudes from Piru be on there.

>MONICA
>I know, I got a ride home though.

>MARCUS
>That's cool.

The bus arrives . . . Marcus and Monica get on it.

INT. BUS, MOVING – DAY

>MONICA
>So, you been jacked?

>MARCUS
>Who the hell told you that?

>MONICA
>Rodney said that some Bloods came up to you last week.

>MARCUS
>Yeah, them fiends always be trying to act hard, but they wouldn't have come up to me if I had one of the homies with me.

>MONICA
>You scared?

>MARCUS
>Man, I won't go that far, but I am looking out for them. The fact that they even came up to me is just messed up.

>MONICA
>Ah, poor baby. You want me to

walk you home?

MARCUS
Nah, it's all good. My homeboy down the street got me something.

MONICA
For real? Lemme see!

Marcus reaches deep into his pocket...

MARCUS
A, but don't be telling people that I got this thing.

. . . and he pulls out *a Swiss Army knife!*

MONICA
(impressed)
That thing is big. You could kill somebody with that.

MARCUS
I ain't trying to kill nobody. I just want people to know that I'm not to be messed with, y'know?

MONICA
I guess.
(beat; then MORE)

MONICA (CONT'D)
Every time I see one of them dudes they're always trying to talk to me.

MARCUS
They just want to get at you, I bet.

Monica playfully punches Marcus on the shoulder.

MARCUS (CONT'D)
Speaking of that, you think I should start talking to Tiffany?

Their playful mood changes; Monica is taken aback by this comment. What does he mean by that? She tries to play it cool . . .

MONICA
Tiffany is a slut. I heard she gave it up to Terrence and Pablo.

MARCUS
Oh, for real? Then hook me up!

Marcus notices the annoyed look on Monica's pretty face:

MARCUS (CONT'D)
Girl, you know I'm just playing.

MONICA
Yeah, but all you nasty boys are going to catch something one of these days. That's why I'm saving myself for marriage.

MARCUS
(laughing)
Whatever, every girl say they going to wait 'til they get married, and them be the girls that's having kids in the 10th grade.

Monica looks away. Why does she bother with this guy anyway?

MONICA
Oh my God.

EXT. HIGH SCHOOL – DAY

The school bus pulls away. A large group of STUDENTS mill around in front of the school waiting for the doors to open. Marcus walks over to his friend, RODNEY. They've known each other for years and immediately fall into familiar conversation:

> RODNEY
> What up Marky-Mark?

> MARCUS
> A, did you tell Monica that I got jacked?

> RODNEY
> A, man . . . she asked.
> (beat; then defensively)
> That girl likes you!

> MARCUS
> You think?

> RODNEY
> HELL NAW! Don't nobody like your ugly a**. You goin'
> straight up die a virgin!

Marcus and Rodney break up laughing.

> MARCUS
> So, what you been working with lately?

> RODNEY
> Monica, she always be on me in class.

> MARCUS
> A, forget you dawg!

> RODNEY
> I'm just messing around.

RICKY, a fellow classmate, walks up and joins in immediately:

> RODNEY (CONT'D)
> You always be so quick to defend this girl, but you ain't even going out.

> RICKY
> A, you know she messing around with Paul, right?

> MARCUS
> What? Who told you that?

> RICKY
> I saw him all hugged up on her yesterday when he was taking her home.

> RODNEY
> Yeah, he does have a car.

> MARCUS
> He's also in the 11th grade *and* is turning 18 next month!

> RODNEY
> A dawg, don't worry about him. He might have a car but that don't mean sh**. He just a pretty boy.

> MARCUS
> What we getting into after school?

> RODNEY
> Shawn and his brother said that they was gonna give us a ride up to the car wash.

MARCUS
For real? That's cool. I ain't got no money and I ain't goin to have none so I might as well try to get paid.

The school BELL RINGS as the DOORS OPEN...

. . . and the STUDENTS begin the endless walk to their first class of the day.

FADE TO:
INT. ALGEBRA CLASS – DAY

As students file in, MS. NERIV begins handing back graded homework.

She passes by Marcus's seat and smiles:

MS. NERIV
Excellent work, Marcus.

Marcus takes the paper from her and notices what is written at the top in big red letters: 96% A!

Not wanting his classmates to see how well he did, Marcus suppresses a smile while quickly shoving the paper into his backpack. *His gangsta image must be maintained at all times!*

FADE TO:
EXT. SCHOOL BASKETBALL COURT – DAY

Marcus and Rodney are joined on the court by their usual group of friends: SHAWN, ANDRE, DEVON, and BIG MIKE—a towering young man with a heart of gold. Although these guys have all known each other for years, tension brews just beneath the surface. The vibe is chilled out and relaxed, but competition hangs in the air.

SHAWN (fair-skinned and tall with long, braided hair), the obvious "leader" of the group, and DEVON, the comedian, has his hand in his pocket:

DEVON
A, where you from?

MARCUS
Man, chill with that.

SHAWN
What's up with you?

RODNEY
Nothing much.

SHAWN
What about them dudes that jacked Marcus?

ANDRE
You want me to handle that for you?

MARCUS
Nah, dog, it's cool. I got something for them the next time I see them.

Marcus carefully pulls out his Swiss Army knife and hands it to Andre.

BIG MIKE
What you going to do with that?

DEVON
What the hell you mean what's he gonna do with it?

Uneasy laughter all around . . . *is Marcus serious about this?*

SHAWN
They probably had burners.

ANDRE
Nah, they didn't have no heat. They just came up to you because you were out walking alone.

RODNEY
Yeah, I figure if he would've had someone else with him he could've taken them real easy.

BIG MIKE
Man, I'm tired of this happening to homies. This is ridiculous.

ANDRE
It's going to keep on happening if we don't get put on.

SHAWN
A, don't start that again. Even if we get put on to a hood, it's just going to get worse.

MARCUS
Yeah, banging on people is a stupid. Don't make no sense.

DEVON
If you heat like me, no one would even come up to you. When they see me coming they know what's up.

The guys all chuckle at Devon's inflated sense of self . . .

RODNEY
Man, shut up. I wouldn't be surprised if some dudes put some serious hands on you!

Rodney grabs the basketball from Shawn and begins dribbling . . . Devon steals it and heads down the court. Marcus is already in place, set up for an easy shot . . . he gets the ball, jumps up, and launches it toward the hoop—the ball hits the rim, misses.

FADE TO:
INT. SCHOOL HALLWAY – DAY

The school day has ended. The noisy hallway is filled with students making after-school plans, gossiping around open lockers while packing up, and getting ready to go home for the day.

Marcus and Shawn make their way through the crowd . . .

SHAWN
You for real with that knife, dawg?
(beat; then MORE)

SHAWN (CONT'D)
Look, these streets don't care about you. They don't care about your brother. They don't care about your mama, neither. Dudes would kill you over five dollars. You can't let them take you from yo' moms and yo' people, man. You too strong for that.

MARCUS
What are you talking about?

74

SHAWN
I'm just saying just run. Yo' kicks and yo' money ain't worth yo' life. My big brother Jason learned the hard way.

MARCUS
I don't know. I just . . . it don't feel right having to live like this. Being afraid of colors. Having brothas killing each other over a female. Having to carry a knife in my pocket to walk to the store.

SHAWN
A, but that's life in the hood. Love it or leave it.

Marcus falls back a step . . .

MARCUS
(to himself)
Leave it.

EXT. HIGH SCHOOL – DAY

Marcus catches up to Shawn as they walk down the front steps of the school . . .

. . . Marcus puts his arm around Shawn's shoulder and they both laugh. A unique bond exists between them; they're brothers in the truest sense of the word... the kind of friends that would take a bullet to save the other one's life.

Waiting at the curb for them is a brand new, shiny, all-black 2005 Cadillac Escalade. Spinning rims, all the options . . . major bling-bling. Sitting behind the wheel is Shawn's older brother, OMAR. Once a street hustler, Omar now owns a successful car wash. He is a respected member of the community, a true success story.

A tinted window is slowly lowered . . .

OMAR
What up, Marc?

MARCUS
Nothing much, just trying to make it up to the Car Wash, make me some money.

OMAR
You ready to put in some work?

MARCUS
Hell yeah—if the money's right.

Omar greets Marcus with an elaborate handshake and a gold-toothed smile.

OMAR
Don't you worry, my man, the money's right.
(beat; then)
The money is right.
(beat; then)
A, Shawn! Get yo' bucket head over here!

Marcus and Shawn jump in the giant SUV and Omar drives off.

INT. ESCALADE, MOVING – DAY

Leather interior, all the options. It's a sweet ride . . .

OMAR
(to Marcus)
I heard somebody been messing
with you.

MARCUS
Yeah, they didn't take much . . .
I ain't tripping.

OMAR
You smart, though. Ain't no
amount of money worth yo life.
Still . . . you can't be letting people take money from you, either.

MARCUS
A, aren't we going to wait for
Rodney?

SHAWN
Yeah, what you doing?

OMAR
Nah . . . we'll catch him tomorrow. There's something I want
to show you first.

EXT. CAR WASH – DAY

Omar pulls up to the Car Wash in a
way that lets everyone know that the
boss has arrived. He parks diagonally
across three spaces as . . . LOLLIPOP
slowly, sensuously washes a Buick in a
skimpy little bikini, exaggerating
every little stroke.

Another scantily-clad female employee
stands out front, arguing with a customer . . . just what kind of a business
is Omar running here?

Omar silently leads Marcus and Shawn
through the lobby . . .

FADE TO:
INT. OMAR'S OFFICE – DAY
Small and cramped, Omar's office is a
disaster area. His entire desk is clut-
tered with stacks of papers. How does
he ever find anything in this mess?

Omar has seated himself in a large,
leather chair behind his desk like a
judge.

Marcus and Shawn stand before him,
listening intently:

OMAR
That stuff that happened to you,
it wasn't right. Ain't nobody
got the right to come up to you,
know what I mean? If some
dude ever come up to Shawn,
I'll blow his head off with a
sawed-off. For real.

Shawn can't hide his embarrassment . . .
as much as he loves and respects Omar,
he doesn't want people to think that he
can't fight his own battles. He too has
an image to maintain.

OMAR (CONT'D)
Y'know, I'm thinking that this
job I got for you will get you up
out the hood so you don't have
to worry about that kind of
thing happening no more.

MARCUS
(unsure of himself)
I'm going to have to start apply-

ing for college soon, so (beat; then looking Omar in the eye) at least with a job maybe they'll take me over some other dude.

OMAR
This . . .
(beat; searching for the right words)
. . . you can't put this sh** on no college application, you feel me?

MARCUS
A, washing cars is a honest profession. No shame.

OMAR
Nah, man. You ain't goin' be washing no damn cars.

MARCUS
(shocked)
What?

Shawn tries to step in and explain:

SHAWN
Yeah, about that . . .

OMAR
You didn't tell him? You two goin to be handing my stuff out at the school.

MARCUS
(excited)
What? Man, I can't be selling no drugs!
(to Shawn)
A, you knew about this?

SHAWN
If I told you, you wouldn't have come up here.

MARCUS
(suddenly quite angry)
We cool and all that, but I can't be doing this up at the school. That stuff'll get me some jail time.

OMAR
Damn! Calm down! If you do what I tell you to do the way I tell you to do it, ain't nothin' gonna happen to you.

Omar reaches in to a desk drawer to pull out a sheet of paper and a pencil.

OMAR (CONT'D)
Look, we gotta be smart about this. You two ain't going to be the ones selling the stuff. You just gotta run it through tutoring.

Marcus and Shawn look confused . . . Omar smiles reassuringly:

OMAR (CONT'D)
Instead of taking the money and giving them the product, one of you takes the money and sends them around to the back of the school to pick up the product. Ya'll going to switch up every hour so nobody knows whose doin' what.

Omar opens another drawer and pulls out a notebook. He sets the notebook down on his desk and opens it. Marcus and Shawn notice something odd—

the center of the notebook's pages have been carved out. No longer a functional notebook, it has become a concealed storage device.

OMAR (CONT'D)
Ya goin' to do this all with notebooks.
(beat; then)
Ya put the product in the notebooks and hand them out during ya tutoring sessions. Ain't no teachers gonna look at these no how, and even if they do—the first few pages are still in place.
(to Marcus)
You a smart kid. Write ya algebra down in there, anything's enough to throw them off.

MARCUS
Man, this is crazy. I can't do this.

OMAR
Look, you want to get out the hood? You want your mama seeing her grandchildren? I lost my little brotha to these streets. Ain't no way I'm losing you and Shawn.
(beat; then MORE)

OMAR (CONT'D)
You goin to make this money and you going to stay low key with it, dig?

MARCUS
You know what you're asking us to do?

OMAR
I'm asking you to make some money. I can't be no clearer than that.

MARCUS
Man . . . I need to think this over. I'll get back to you on this . . .

Omar gets up from his chair, walks over to Marcus.

OMAR
Don't keep me waiting. There's a bunch of fiends at your school that want to be put on. If you ain't on board, that's cool. Someone else can take ya place.
(beat; then MORE)
I only brought ya into it because we been down for a long time.

EXT. CAR WASH – DAY

Marcus storms out of the car wash looking like he's just seen a ghost. Hands in his pockets, head down . . . *what to do?* Shawn follows out behind him, trying to catch up.

SHAWN
A, hold up!

MARCUS
Man, I can't believe you got me into this. How the hell are we supposed to sell drugs at the school?

SHAWN
I don't like it none either, but if we put Devon on it then there

won't be no problems.

MARCUS
Nah, man. I can't do this. I can't do it. We'd end up goin' to jail, Shawn! Jail!

SHAWN
That's not why you don't want to do it. You just scared somebody going to jack you for you stuff. That's why.

Marcus turns around and SHOVES Shawn, nearly knocking him to the ground.

SHAWN
You know I'm right . . . You can't tell me no different. It's okay to be scared. You ain't got to do this if you don't want to. I won't hate you, Omar won't hate you. You just scared, it's okay.

Marcus turns and walks away, leaving Shawn on the sidewalk . . .

SHAWN (CONT'D)
You can't even pull out that knife! You ain't cut out to be no pusher!

FADE TO:
EXT. MARCUS'S HOME, STREET – DAY

Marcus walks down the street he grew up on, lost in thought.

He looks up just in time to see Monica getting out of a flashy car driven by PAUL—an eighteen year old, good-looking playa—everything that Marcus is not. Monica lingers a moment too long and Paul takes the opportunity to KISS her.

Marcus looks away, disgusted.

CUT TO:
INT. MARCUS'S HOME, LIVING ROOM - DAY

DOMINIQUE, Marcus's thirteen-year-old younger brother, sits on the floor engrossed in a video game.

Marcus walks in and sits down on the couch.

MARCUS
What's up?

DOMINIQUE
Level 12 is hard.

MARCUS
I told you—first beat the little guys, then kill the boss.

DOMINIQUE
Fo' sho, fo' sho.
(beat; then)
A, was that Monica outside just now?

He knows it was her . . .

MARCUS
Yeah. So what about it?

DOMINIQUE
Who was that she was with?

. . . he's just trying to get a reaction out of Marcus.

MARCUS
Man, don't worry about that.

DOMINIQUE
Your girl is out with some other
dude? Now that's hilarious!

Marcus stays cool . . . he grabs the
video game controller away from his
little brother.

Dominique tries to resist but it's no use.
Marcus is bigger, faster, and stronger.

MARCUS
A, leave me alone, you ain't got
no girls up at the middle school.

DOMINIQUE
You love to hate on a brotha.

MARCUS
Whatever.
(beat; then)
Where's mom at?

DOMINIQUE
She at the store. You still haven't
told her about what happened?
You was supposed to buy milk
for us with that money.

Marcus stops playing the video game.

Suddenly serious, he looks his younger
brother straight in the eye:

MARCUS
I'd rather have her be mad at
me because she thought I lost it
than admit that somebody
jacked me.
(beat; then softly)

I don't want that on her heart.

DOMINIQUE
But what happens next time
they come up to you? You just
let them take yo' money? Our
money? The money we need for
groceries?

MARCUS
(suddenly angry)
Since when did you think about
us?

Marcus gets up and LEAVES.

DOMINIQUE
Since mama told me she had to
get another job!

We hear a DOOR SLAM.

CUT TO:
INT. MARCUS'S BEDROOM – DAY

Marcus lies on his bed, staring at the
spinning ceiling fan... around and
around and around, like the thoughts
in his head.

A KNOCK on his bedroom window—
it's Monica!

Marcus raises the window and helps
Monica pull herself in.

MARCUS
What are you doing here?

MONICA
I just wanted to tell you that
Tommy is coming home.

MARCUS
Tommy?

MONICA
I can't believe I didn't tell you
before. I completely forget that
he gets out this month.
(beat; then)
I guess I've been a little caught
up . . .

MARCUS
(interrupting, angry)
With Paul?

Monica stares at him silently. *How did
Marcus know?*

MARCUS (CONT'D)
When'd you start going out?

MONICA
A while ago . . .

MARCUS
"A while ago?" A known Blood
is going out with my homegirl
and I don't even know about it?!

MONICA
It ain't like that. We just started
going out.

MARCUS
Didn't he go to Juvy?

MONICA
He's changed.
(beat; then)
He's doing better in school now.

MARCUS
What about Tommy? He ain't

goin' to stand for him all
hugged up on you!

MONICA
Tommy can't tell me what to
do! Besides, Tommy was cool
with Paul back when they was
kicking it in Inglewood.

Monica stops herself, realizes something.

Marcus is really upset.

She sits down on the bed, motions for
Marcus to sit next to her. He ignores
her invitation, remains standing:

MONICA (CONT'D)
I'm just telling you because I
know that Tommy was your
boy. With him out, you might
not get jacked any more.

Marcus looks away . . . hurt, angry, and
confused.

FADE TO:
INT. MARCUS'S HOME, KITCHEN
– EARLY MORNING

Every square inch of the kitchen table is
covered with heaping plates of food:
ham, eggs, bacon, pancakes, cereal.
There's enough here to feed a small
army. Marcus and Dominique are seated, grazing like animals. The smiles on
their faces say it all: *this is good eating!*

TERESA, Forty years old, enters the
room. She is visibly exhausted but her
kind face lights up when she sees her
boys enjoying themselves.

TERESA
I see you two like what you see!

MARCUS
Thanks, mama. I'm about to kill a whole plate of bacon.

Teresa walks up behind Marcus, gently putting her hands on his shoulders.

TERESA
Not so fast. We need to talk.

MARCUS
Mama, you still trippin' over that milk money?

TERESA
Dom told me about what happened.

Marcus's shoulders stiffen.

TERESA (CONT'D)
Son, why didn't you tell me that some boys took your money?

MARCUS
I couldn't, mama! I couldn't tell you no stuff like that. You'd have been heartbroken!

TERESA
It was only a couple of dollars. That's not going to hurt us.

Teresa's hands slowly move up to rub Marcus's head . . . she loves him so much, it's obvious that she'd do anything for him.

TERESA (CONT'D)
. . . But you not telling me when you have problems does.

Marcus realizes something. He stops eating and looks down:

MARCUS
Is that why you cooked?

TERESA
I know that you've been saving up for grocery money by not eating lunch and I don't want my child having to worry about my finances.

MARCUS
But, mama . . .

Teresa puts her fingers to her lips . . . Shhhh!

MARCUS
Don't you have to get another job?

TERESA
(smiling proudly)
I'm your mother and your father, sweetheart. It's only natural that I would have to take up two jobs.

FADE TO:
EXT. MARCUS'S HOME, STREET – DAY

Marcus walks toward the bus stop with a renewed sense of purpose. Something has changed . . . he seems to be at peace with himself.

The same car that Monica got out of the day before suddenly pulls up to the curb.

The passenger window lowers and Paul

beckons Marcus to come over:

PAUL
Get in.

Marcus freezes. He's about to turn away when he realizes that Paul is aiming the barrel of a Tech-49 directly at him.

Marcus opens the door and gets in . . .

. . . Paul squeals away from the curb.

INT. PAUL'S CAR, MOVING – DAY

The interior of Paul's Pimp-Mobile is ridiculous. The furry dice dangling from the rearview mirror are a nice touch. The ladies must love it...

PAUL
How long you been talking to Monica?

So . . . *that's* what this is about. Marcus braces himself for the worst:

MARCUS
I've known her since we were in elementary school, homie. We just friends.

Paul smiles as if he and Marcus were suddenly best friends . . .

PAUL
She told me what happened.

. . . Marcus is too scared to react.

PAUL (CONT'D)
To you. She told me what happened to you. I just want to have my girl's back, y'know? If she not happy, I'm not happy.

Paul waits for a reaction from Marcus—there is none.

PAUL (CONT'D)
I'm saying, I know the fools who got you. We can go handle that if you want to.

MARCUS
Serious?

PAUL
Yeah, my girl is worried about you, keeps saying she wants me to pick you up everyday. Now I ain't wit that, but . . . I am wit getting those dudes that hit you up. Same dudes got my boy, Two-Time, the other day . . . same day they got you.
(beat; then)
So . . . you wanna get put on, blood?

Marcus doesn't trust Paul at all. Where is he driving to, anyway? This is not the way to school! The whole situation has gotten out of control.

MARCUS
Look, man. I ain't down with that. I can't be killing nobody. Just tell Monica that I'll be OK.

PAUL
I'm tryin' put you on the game. You ain't goin' make it in these streets without my help.

MARCUS
I respect what you and Monica got going on, really I do, but I just

can't be part of no gang-banging.

Paul pulls over to the side of the road . . .

> PAUL
> Forget you then. See what I care
> bout yo' punk.

. . . and opens the door.

Marcus gets out. Paul gives him the finger and speeds away.

FADE TO:
EXT. HIGH SCHOOL - DAY

Marcus runs up the front stairs, out of breath. He is late and the door is locked. This means one thing: detention. *Damn!*

CUT TO:
INT. HIGH SCHOOL STUDY HALL – DAY

The students are clustered around large tables. MARCUS, RODNEY, and ANDRE all sit together talking in hushed tones. The TEACHER watching study hall today is too busy correcting homework to even notice.

> ANDRE
> You for real? Guess that means
> Paul ain't getting any from
> Monica yet.

> RODNEY
> So . . . what you goin' do?

> MARCUS
> Keep this on the low . . .
> (Marcus looks around cautiously;
> then)

Me and Shawn are going to be sellin' out the school.

> RODNEY
> What'chu mean?

> MARCUS
> Omar goin' supply us and we
> goin' sell it to the students.

> ANDRE
> Since when?

> MARCUS
> Since yesterday.

> RODNEY
> (realizing something)
> That's why you leave me behind
> yesterday?

> MARCUS
> Omar said you wasn't going to
> be ready yet. Me and Shawn goin'
> sell first, then we see about you.

Silence as Andrew and Rodney process this news.

> ANDRE
> You sure about this?

CUT TO:
EXT. HIGH SCHOOL - DAY

Students pour out of the school, glad that the day has ended. Buses line up in front to take them home. Devon and Shawn are walking along as Marcus runs up to join them . . .

> DEVON
> Damn, you stupid for not doing
> it. It's easy money.

MARCUS
Change of plans, homie. I'm in.

Shawn stops walking, looks Marcus in the eye—

SHAWN
Fo sho?

—there's no going back.

Marcus nods . . . his decision has been made.

SHAWN (CONT'D)
Alright then. I see you grown yourself a pair!

Devon realizes that this means he is out—

DEVON
(protesting)
Damn, dawg! I ain't goin' punk out on you like this.

SHAWN
(interrupting)
I don't need you, see?
(beat; then)
Omar said he didn't want to put nobody on that he couldn't trust. Wait a while, let's see what happens.

Devon walks away, defeated . . . he turns around one last time:

DEVON
Alright, but remember—IMA HUSTLA, IMA IMA HUSTLA, HOMIE!

FADE TO:
EXT. LIQUOR STORE – DAY

A typical corner liquor store. Several of the windows are boarded up, trash blows across the sidewalk in front. Marcus and Shawn walk up . . .

INT. LIQUOR STORE – DAY

Marcus and Shawn stand in front of the reach-in cooler trying to decide on a soda. Grape? Orange? Too many choices . . .

MARCUS
A, how much you goin' to make doing this?

SHAWN
On the real, 'bout a grand a week.

MARCUS
Real talk?

SHAWN
You know.

They reach in and make their selections: Strawberry Fanta! On their way up to the front counter, THREE MEN burst into the store wearing ski masks! Each of them holds a gun—T'S A STICK-UP!

FIRST MAN
You know what this is, give me all the money!

The nervous CLERK fumbles with cash register, can't get it open . . .

. . . Marcus and Shawn try to hide behind a giant display of Doritos.

SECOND MAN
Come on! We ain't got all day!

A bag of chips drops to the floor—
one of the men turns around, aiming
his gun directly at Marcus and Shawn!

THIRD MAN
Get out here!

Marcus and Shawn walk to the front of
the store. They are both terrified.

One of the robbers lowers his gun . . .

SECOND MAN
Marcus? Is that you?

MARCUS
Huh?

The second man takes off his ski mask—
and he turns out to be Tommy,
Monica's older brother . . . newly
released from jail.

TOMMY
Damn, you grown up now! Even
got some hair on yo' chin.

*What's going on? Isn't this supposed to be a
robbery?*

FIRST MAN
Is you stupid?

TOMMY
This is my little homie right
here. (beat; then full of pride)
He's the little brother I never
had!

The bewildered CLERK hands over the
cash, fistfuls of it.

THIRD MAN
Let's get the hell out of here!

CUT TO:
INT. TOMMY'S GETWAY CAR,
MOVING – DAY

TOMMY, MARCUS, and SHAWN are
crammed in the front seat. The other
two robbers are in the back seat, counting the money and smoking a blunt.

Marcus and Shawn are still in a state of
shock . . .

TOMMY
What? They did what?

MARCUS
They took my mama's money. I
was on my way to the grocery
store . . .
(beat; then)
I think they was from Piru.

TOMMY
Yeah, they was really thirsty.
(beat; then)
Marcus, whatever you need, you
know I got you. Me and you
been down since elementary,
dawg. Where you headed?

CUT TO:
EXT. CAR WASH – DAY

Tommy's car pulls up and the door
opens. Marcus, Shawn, and an enormous
cloud of smoke exit the vehicle . . .

CUT TO:
INT. OMAR'S OFFICE – DAY

Omar is seated behind his desk like Al Pacino in *Scarface*. His shiny jewelry sparkles under the fluorescent lighting as a smile slowly creeps across his face . . .

> OMAR
> I knew you'd come to your senses.

Marcus looks like he's just been punched in the kidneys.

> OMAR (CONT'D)
> Now, let's step in to my real office.

Omar pushes his desk aside to reveal a hatch in the floor—he opens the hatch, motioning for Marcus and Shawn to climb down.

CUT TO:
Blackness . . .

. . . A LIGHT FLICKERS ON, revealing:

INT. OMAR'S BASEMENT – DAY

A small dusty room, just big enough for three people. The walls are lined with dozens of large packages wrapped in brown paper. Smaller packets of cocaine are clearly visible in Zip-Lock baggies.

Marcus and Shawn are way out of their league.

> OMAR
> You never can be too careful, know what I mean? Only the people that's really down with me even know where the prod-uct is otherwise they'd be trying

to steal from me, dig?
> (beat; then)
> But you two are family. I know I won't have to worry about any of my stuff coming up missing, right?

> SHAWN
> Nope.

Omar picks up three packets of the white powder and puts them in one of Shawn's coat pockets . . .

> MARCUS
> Nah, we cool.

. . . he picks up three more packets and does the same for Marcus.

> OMAR
> That's what I want to hear.
> (beat; then)
> Like I said, you gotta be smart, you know? If ya'll get caught with this, I trust I won't hear my name come up now, will I?

> SHAWN
> You my brother. I'd die for you, you know that.

Marcus is not at all comfortable with this arrangement. The reality of what he is about to do hits him with the power of a speeding train . . .

> OMAR
> What about you? I'm putting you up on some real game right here. You ready to get this money?

MARCUS
Fo' sho!

Omar smiles and offers him an elaborate handshake which turns into a sort of manly hug—

—but Omar quickly pulls away:

OMAR
One more thing.

Omar reaches into his pocket, pulls out a HANDGUN. Marcus's eyes widen at the sight of the smooth, black steel. Omar hands the piece over to Shawn.

SHAWN
For me?

OMAR
You can never be too careful . . .
(beat; then)
All you need to do is flash it. Nobody goin' kill themselves for some dime bags.

SHAWN
What about Marcus?

Marcus was afraid this might happen. He holds his breath—

OMAR
Ya'll goin' be together so you only need one piece for right now.

—and let's out a huge sigh of relief. He's never even held a gun, much less fired one.

OMAR (CONT'D)
You start tomorrow and all I got to say is this: don't mess it up.

(beat; then smiling)
Now get the hell outta here.

INSERT MONTAGE:

Marcus and Shawn are very good at their new job—maybe too good! They're an instant success as . . .

. . . CRACK-HEADS approach Marcus in front of the school, desperate for a fix. Money is exchanged, and they are directed back to Shawn who is waiting with the product.

This process repeats itself again and again, many times in quick succession—

—and as NEW CUSTOMERS begin showing up, THE WAD OF CASH in Shawn's pocket continues to grow and expand.

Marcus and Shawn sit in Omar's office, hundred dollar bills fanned out on the desk in an obscene display of instant wealth. Omar smiles while raking it all into a drawer and . . .

. . . the CRACK-HEADS keep coming back for more. Business booms, it's hard to keep up with the market's demand.

Marcus has a hard time staying awake in class. His teacher, MS. NERIV sadly shakes her head as she hands back a test. At the top of the page, in red, is the grade: C-

But the MONEY keeps rolling in . . .

. . . and RODNEY goes to work for

88

Omar as well and they're no longer just selling to the usual assortment of CRACK-HEADS and STREET PEOPLE—

—THEY'RE SELLING IN THE SCHOOL itself: classrooms, hallways, it doesn't matter. Omar's Three Musketeers are bold and will do business anywhere because the amount of cash they're seeing is truly amazing—$15,000? $20,000? More, much more . . .

. . . and there's no end in sight.

FADE TO:
INT. MARCUS'S HOME, KITCHEN – DAY

Marcus walks in with a large bag of groceries, smiling. Dominique and Teresa are sitting at the table.

Teresa looks like she's been up all night crying.

DOMINIQUE
A, you got those cookies?

MARCUS
Man, I got you, I got you.

TERESA
Marcus, honey . . .
(beat; then)
You've been bringing in groceries almost every other day.

MARCUS
Mama, what kind of man would I be if I didn't help take care of us? I told you, once I got this job I was gonna help out round here.

TERESA
How much you making up at that car wash?

Marcus tries to smile, suddenly uncomfortable.

MARCUS
Mama . . .

TERESA
(interrupting)
What do you do up there to be getting paid so much money?

MARCUS
Omar is just . . . Look, he knows times are tough and he just hooking all of us up.

TERESA
I worry about you, son.

MARCUS
Mama, I know what I'm doing. I just gotta make sure stuff around here is taken care of since Daddy ain't 'round no more.

A single tear rolls down Teresa's face—

TERESA
It's so hard . . .

—Marcus and Dominique both notice and move in to hug her tightly.

TOGETHER THEY ARE A FAMILY, AN UNSTOPPABLE TEAM. Nothing will ever change that fact and each of them is keenly aware of just how much they rely on each other.

MARCUS
We here for you, mama.

The moment stands still and Marcus wishes it would never end.

FADE TO:
EXT. HIGH SCHOOL – DAY

Marcus and Shawn walk together on their daily beat behind the school, business as usual.

MARCUS
This is crazy, man. I ain't never seen so much money in my life. How much we make last week?

SHAWN
Six, maybe seven grand.

MARCUS
For real?

Before Shawn can answer, BIG MIKE walks up to them—

BIG MIKE
A man, what's up?

—looking to score.

MARCUS
Nothing much. You know, trying to get this money.

BIG MIKE
I want you to hook me up.

MARCUS
What?

Marcus looks over to Shawn. They've already sold to kids at the school, but selling to their friends is a bridge they have yet to cross.

BIG MIKE
Give me some Yayo, dawg. I hear you got the hookup.

MARCUS
Have you lost your damn mind? Do you know what it does to people?

Big Mike grabs Marcus and spins him around. His eyes blink wildly, he's shaking . . .

. . . at that moment Marcus realizes just how serious his friend's problem is.

Big Mike reaches into his pocket and pulls out a wad of cash. By now he's shaking so badly that most of it falls to the ground.

BIG MIKE
That's four hundred, take it.

Marcus and Shawn are stunned. *What next?*

BIG MIKE (CONT'D)
Man, I need something. I ain't been doin' well in school, my little sister is out with this Mexican fool every night . . .
(beat; then)
I can't take it no more. I need something to get me through it all.

MARCUS
Damn, man. I can't . . .

BIG MIKE
(screaming desperately)

I NEED THIS!

Shawn nods to Marcus . . . *go ahead, do it.*

Marcus hands Big Mike the hollowed-out notebook he got from Omar . . .

MARCUS
Remember, study as much as possible.

. . . Big Mike grabs it and runs off, desperate for a fix.

FADE TO:
INT. HIGH SCHOOL LUNCH-ROOM – DAY

MARCUS, SHAWN, RODNEY, DEVON, and ANDRE are all sitting together. Everyone has a healthy appetite except for Marcus who has barely touched his sandwich.

ANDRE
You sold it to him?

MARCUS
What else was I gonna do? He was desperate.

SHAWN
Damn . . . I didn't know.

RODNEY
We can't let him get hooked on the blow. He goin' end up like that 12th grader who messed around wit dirty needles and caught the bug.

DEVON
If he wanna do drugs, let him do drugs.

(beat; then)
He knows what it does.
(beat; then)
We can't tell him what to do.

MARCUS
If anything happens to him, it'll be my fault. We can't just let this fly.
(beat; then)
I can't . . .

SHAWN
I hear you, but money is money. If this dude is slipping us hundreds there ain't much we can do about that.

MARCUS
I can't believe my ears. Don't you care bout your homie?

SHAWN
You knew what would happen but you still sold it to him!

Marcus gets up from the table and walks away without a word.

SHAWN (CONT'D)
Yeah, that's what I thought.

FADE TO:
EXT. MULTIPLEX CINEMA – NIGHT

Bright lights, long lines . . . everyone loves going to the movies!

FADE IN:
INT. CINEMA – NIGHT

People are taking their seats, waiting

for the movie to begin. A group of teenagers are throwing popcorn at the MIDDLE-AGED MAN sitting by himself. Waves of laughter pierce the auditorium as Marcus and Andre sit towards the back, deep in discussion.

ANDRE
You still getting paid, right?

MARCUS
Fo' sho.

ANDRE
You a right big baller now.

MARCUS
I'm doin' alright.

The lights dim and as the previews finally start to roll . . .

. . . Monica, and her two friends, RHODESIA and MARIANNA, walk down the aisle.

MARCUS
Monica?

MONICA
Long time no see. What's been going on with you?

MARCUS
Nothing much, just chilling with my homie, Andre.

Monica glances over at Andre and walks over to him.

MONICA
Hey Andre . . .

Monica gives Andre a big hug, hoping

to get Marcus's attention.

RHODESIA
So, this the dude that's been slanging up at the school, huh?

MARIANNA
Yeah, him and my baby, Shawn.

Baby?

MARCUS
Marianna, Shawn has a girl-friend.

MARIANNA
I know, me.

Marcus shrugs. He moves over one seat so Rhodesia can sit next to Andre. Monica sits on the other side of him, and Marianna next to Monica.

MONICA
Hey, what's up?

. . . Marcus ignores her.

MONICA (CONT'D)
How come you been ducking me for the past month and a half?

MARCUS
I ain't been ducking you.

MONICA
Yeah, right.
(beat; then)
Look, I'm worried about you.

MARCUS
Well, I'm fine. I got money, I'm happy. My mama's happy, we got

groceries. It's all good, Monica.
(beat; then)
You don't need to worry about
me.

MONICA
You been hanging around
Tommy?

MARCUS
I seen him around.

MONICA
Tommy saw Paul picking me up
and he come out with a baseball
bat, talking about how he was
goin' to get him for snitching.

MARCUS
Yeah, that's my dawg.
(beat; then)
Tommy.

MONICA
Look at you . . . you been selling for how long, and you
weren't even going to tell me?

MARCUS
Monica, I didn't want anybody
to know.

MONICA
I'm not just anybody, Marcus.
(beat; then)
Besides, everybody does know.

Marcus considers this in silence . . .
could it be?
On the movie screen, Vin Diesel is
fighting a monster with six eyeballs
and eight arms.

FADE TO:
EXT. MULTIPLEX CINEMA –
NIGHT

MARCUS, MONICA, RHODESIA,
ANDRE, and MARIANNA are all
standing outside the movie theater
waiting for their rides.

MONICA
Marianna, how are you getting
home?

MARIANNA
My baby is coming to get me.

As soon as she finishes her sentence,
Shawn pulls up in a 1974 Volkswagen:
tires almost flat, exhaust pipe falling
off, fender bent . . .

SHAWN
What up Marcus!

MARCUS
With all that money, this is all
you could afford?

SHAWN
Don't hate, it only needs to
drive, I don't need to be flossing.

MARIANNA
That's right, baby!

ANDRE
Shawn, you have a girl. What
happened?

SHAWN
Her pops said that I wasn't a
"decent young man." I told her
that we could still be together,

but she told me to cut them braids off so he'll accept me. I told her I ain't changing who I am, especially for no female.
(beat; then)
Alright, get yo' fine self in this car!

Monica reaches for her cellular phone and dials a number

MONICA
Paul baby, you gonna come pick me up?

Marcus is disgusted by this sudden turn of events. *She needs to leave right now!*

MONICA (CONT'D)
What? Is that all you care about?
(beat; then disgusted)
Why? Why are you doing this to me?

Monica puts down the phone, too shocked to cry.

MARCUS
Monica? What did he say?

MONICA
I can't believe he would...

Monica drifts off, unable to complete the sentence.

Marcus seizes the moment:

MARCUS
Look, let's just go home. I'll walk with you.

Monica is on the verge of tears.

MONICA
Thanks.

CUT TO:

EXT. MARCUS'S HOUSE - NIGHT

Monica walks up to Marcus's doorstep.

MONICA
Can I kick it at your house for a while? Just, until my mom gets home?

MARCUS
Yeah, come on in.

INT. MARCUS'S HOUSE – NIGHT

Monica sits on Marcus's couch, hands still firmly gripped to her cell phone. Marcus turns out the Television set to an episode of *The Cosby Show.*

MONICA
I just can't believe he talked to me that way . . .

MARCUS
What did he say?

MONICA
Some stuff about how I need to put out . . .

MARCUS
That dude is foul! If you can't see that—

MONICA
(interrupting)
I know from what you see he just looks like some dude, but . . .

Defending Paul has become so

ingrained in Monica's mind that she almost can't help herself . . .

. . . Marcus goes in for the kill:

> MARCUS
> I saw him messing around with Nancy at the mall yesterday. I didn't want to tell you because I thought you would've figured it out by now.

> MONICA
> No . . . no!

> MARCUS
> Monica, you deserve better than that dude. I'm not perfect but I would never dog out my girl like that.

During all of this, Marcus has somehow managed to get his arm all the way around Monica's shoulder. He draws her near, a comforting shoulder to cry on.

> MONICA
> I'm just so confused right now. I thought he was different.

> MARCUS
> Maybe different isn't what you need right now.
> (beat; then)
> Maybe what you need is someone who's always been there for you.

Marcus's hands begin to wander—

> MONICA
> Marcus . . .

—and soon his mouth is on hers. They kiss passionately, softly on the mouth.

Marcus tries to put a hand up her shirt. Monica freezes—

> MARCUS
> I love you. Always, I've loved you.

—he knows the magic words.

In the background Bill Cosby can be heard giving advice to his adoring family.

FADE TO BLACK
INT. MARCUS'S BEDROOM – DAY

Marcus wakes up from a deep sleep to find THE BARREL OF A SHOTGUN pointing in his face!

Omar is standing over him, a crazed look on his face . . .

> OMAR
> Get up! We gotta handle some business!

> MARCUS
> (not yet awake)
> What?

> OMAR
> GET UP!

CUT TO:
INT. ESCALADE, MOVING – DAY

Shawn, dressed entirely in black, sits in the back seat . . . cool as ice.
Marcus rides up front with Omar.

> OMAR
> This is some real sh** we about to get into.

> MARCUS
> A, man, where's Monica?

OMAR
Don't worry bout her. She next door. I woke her up first, told her to be on her way.

MARCUS
Man, what's going on?

OMAR
Seems somebody thought it was cool to just get all up in my stash like it wasn't nothing. I know it wasn't one of you, but it was one of yo homies that did it.

SHAWN
Aw man, how do figure?

OMAR
One of my girls said they saw that big black brotha that ya'll been hanging out with and some other dude run up in there and steal my product.
(beat; then)
I put two and two together and figure out that you two the only ones who could've told him where I keep the product.

MARCUS
You talkin' 'bout Big Mike? Man, I didn't—

OMAR
(interrupting)
A, forget all that noise. Since you the ones who caused this, you the ones who goin finish it.

Marcus and Shawn stare at him, uncomprehending.

OMAR (CONT'D)
We goin' to get my blow back and smoke this fool!

Omar reaches under his seat—

MARCUS
Man, I can't do this. I can't do this!

—and pulls out an AK-47.

OMAR
You ain't got no choice in the matter! You either get down or get put down. Now, you ready to own up?

SHAWN
Dawg, can't we just get the product back?

OMAR
You too? Damn! You know better than anybody that any fool that steals from Omar's gonna get his whole grill lit up.
(beat; then)
Stop acting like a couple of punks and handle this sh**!

EXT. CRACK HOUSE, INGLE-WOOD – DAY

The black Escalade pulls up and screeches to a halt. OMAR, SHAWN, and MARCUS jump out of the vehicle and storm the house—

—Omar cocks his rifle:

OMAR
Knock, knock!

> VOICE (O.S.)
> Who is you?

Omar fires a shell directly in to the door.

> OMAR
> The gingerbread man!

Omar kicks the door in and shoots two men in the face.

Their heads EXPLODE—

—as Marcus and Shawn cringe in disgust.

A MAN runs up to Shawn with a knife in his hand!

Shawn reacts quickly and the man goes down screaming in pain.

Shawn shoots him again just to be sure.

Marcus, holding the AK-47, slowly makes his way up the stairs . . .

. . . and down the hall—

—he KICKS OPEN A DOOR and sees Big Mike and two other CRACK-HEADS, completely naked and high on the stolen cocaine.

> MARCUS
> Big Mike! Why you doin' this, man?

> CRACKHEAD
> Screw you and Omar!

The Crack-head reaches for a gun, but . . . his reflexes aren't sharp enough—

—and Marcus shoots him in the stomach.

> BIG MIKE
> (terrified, about to cry)
> I needed to get high, man! I couldn't help myself.

Omar runs up behind Marcus.

> OMAR
> Marc, lay them out!

> MARCUS
> Omar . . . I . . . Big Mike is—
> Omar aims his gun directly at Marcus's head.

> OMAR
> (very calmly)
> Lay them out or I lay you out.
> (beat; then gesturing toward Big Mike)
> And your little ho.

Marcus shoots Big Mike and the remaining crack-head.

> OMAR (CONT'D)
> (smiling)
> Get the product and let's go.

Unable to move even a muscle, Marcus stands still in utter shock and disbelief. I just killed three men . . . *I took three lives. I'm going to hell. Naw, I'm already in hell.*

> OMAR (CONT'D)
> I said let's go!

Shawn enters the room, out of breath from running—

> SHAWN
> We gotta go . . .

—and is horrified by the blood and carnage.

> SHAWN (CONT'D)
> Man, what the hell? Mike? Big Mike!

> OMAR
> Forget it, Shawn. Grab the blow, Marcus. Get to the car.

FADE TO:
INT. ESCALADE, MOVING – DAY

OMAR, SHAWN, and MARCUS speed away from the slaughter, their clothes splattered with fresh blood.

The missing cocaine has been recovered and Omar is in good spirits.

> OMAR
> You did good, you both did good.
> (beat; then)
> You first time, huh?

Omar beams ear to ear like a proud papa . . .

. . . Marcus and Shawn are yet to fully grasp exactly what it was they did. *How did this happen?*

CUT TO:
INT. MARCUS'S BEDROOM – DAY
Marcus throws himself onto the bed, face down . . . AND SOBS AS IF THE WORLD WERE COMING TO AN END.

FADE TO:
INT. ANDRE'S LIVINGROOM –

AFTERNOON

MARCUS faces ANDRE and DEVON, on Andre's living room floor.

> ANDRE
> How the hell could you do this?! How could you Kill Big Mike?!

Andre is on the verge of tears. Andre's Colt 49 is pointed at his forehead.

> ANDRE
> But, you goin' always be my homie.
> I'm ready to ride for you if you really want to get out this s***.

> MARCUS
> Dre…

> ANDRE
> Let's go get Omar.

FADE TO:
EXT. CAR WASH – NIGHT

ANDRE, RODNEY, and MARCUS huddle in the shadows of the car wash.

The lights are out and the business is closed.

Omar's black Escalade is parked out front which can only mean one thing:

OMAR IS IN HIS OFFICE.

> DEVON
> (to Marcus)
> We dawgs for life. What you did was bad, dude, real bad. You killed the homie Big Mike . . .

but we goin' get you and Shawn out of this.
(beat; then)
Even if that means we gotta die.

RODNEY
That's right. We got out there. Soldiers for life!

ANDRE
Ya ready to go set it off?

MARCUS
Chea, let's ride.

Marcus and his crew boldly march through the front doors . . .

CUT TO:
INT. OMAR'S OFFICE – NIGHT

The door nearly flies off its hinges as Marcus and company file in to Omar's messy office.

Seated in the chair is Shawn . . . his feet kicked up on the desk. *He couldn't be happier!*

SHAWN
What's up?

ANDRE
We here to get you out of this! You need to quit—

SHAWN
(interrupts, laughing)
We in this fo' life. There ain't no way out.
(beat; then)
Marcus and Rodney knows that.

MARCUS
Shawn, we killed . . . I killed Big Mike.

SHAWN
He had it coming. Anybody who messes with Omar the King, gets dropped.

MARCUS
Look, I'll talk to Omar . . .

Shawn rises from the chair—

SHAWN
What? You want out now? You and me are s'pose to be homies, and you goin' abandon me after all we've been through?

—and gets directly in Marcus's face.

MARCUS
I can't live like this anymore. I can't do it, Shawn.

Shawn tries to stare Marcus down but he's weak and everyone in the room knows it. *Without Omar around to defend him, Shawn's bark is much worse than his bite.*

Sensing the shift in power, Shawn relents and opens the hatch.

SHAWN
(smiling weakly)
You goin' to die anyway. Be my guest.

Marcus is the first to go down . . . the others follow quickly behind.

CUT TO:
INT. OMAR'S CELLAR DRUG LAB
– NIGHT

Omar is sitting on an upturned crate, shotgun in hand, sniffing wildly. Nostrils flared, he blinks like a maniac. His teeth are grinding out of control.

It looks like Omar may be his own best customer!

MARCUS, ANDRE, DEVON, and RODNEY move in. Omar is surrounded, trapped like an animal.

> OMAR
> What up? Ya'll wanna celebrate? We got our sh** back!

> MARCUS
> It's over, Omar. I'm done.

> OMAR
> What the hell do you mean you're done? All I've ever done was try to help you! I got you this job, I made sure you was safe. You owe me!

> RODNEY
> We just want out, Omar. We'll give you back all the money, all the drugs—we just want to be done with this!

Omar SHOOTS Rodney in the chest with the shotgun.

> OMAR
> I run this show! You in my basement! You in my lab! If I say jump, you say how high!

> ANDRE
> I'm goin' kill you!

Andres shoots at Omar!

Omar dodges the bullets and returns fire, hitting Andre in the leg.

Andre screams out in pain!

> MARCUS
> Enough, man!

> OMAR
> You brought this upon yourself! You were my soldier and you disobeyed a direct order. In my eyes that's grounds for a court martial! Consider yourself officially reprimanded and relieved of your duties as an officer in my army!

Omar cocks the rifle and aims it directly at Marcus's head.

> OMAR (CONT'D)
> Any last words?

Marcus closes his eyes and prepares for the—

WITHOUT WARNING, TOMMY BURSTS IN TO THE BASEMENT SURPRISING EVERYONE!

> TOMMY
> You ain't goin' take out my little man like this!

Omar shoots him in the chest—

and Tommy goes down hard.

Omar laughs and reloads the rifle.

OMAR
You were my ace . . . you were my road dog . . . I didn't want it to end . . .

Tommy quickly sits up and SHOOTS OMAR IN THE HEAD.

MARCUS
Tommy!

Everyone is in a state of shock. What just happened?

TOMMY
Bulletproof vest. Never leave home without it!

FADE TO:
EXT. GREYHOUND BUS STATION – DAY

Marcus and Monica stand on the platform. Behind them, passengers have already begun boarding.

MONICA
You sure you have to go?

MARCUS
Mama said it was for the best. She says the only way I can turn my life around is if I go to where no one knows me. She said I need to reinvent myself...

MONICA
I'm coming to see you. We'll be together. I'll get a job, and . . .

MARCUS
(interrupting)
I want you to be happy, and that can't happen as long as you're mixed up with a dude like me.

MONICA
But Marcus, that's not true.

MARCUS
There's nothing to discuss.
(beat; then)
I love you and because I love you we can't ever be together. I took another person's life and for that I am very sorry, but . . . I can't ever be the man you need me to be.

Marcus grabs Monica and goes in for one last kiss—

—and it's a kiss that neither of them will ever forget.

FADE TO:
INT. GREYHOUND BUS, DRIVING – DAY

Marcus takes a blank writing journal out of his bag and lays it across his lap . . .

. . . he pauses briefly before carefully writing down the first line:

"THE STORY OF MARCUS HENDERSON: THE LAST DAY OF TOMORROW"
FADE OUT.

IT TAKES A VILLAGE TO RAISE A CHILD
LASHANEE KING

We all go through changes in our lives. Sometimes those changes may change *your* life so dramatically that they begin to affect all of those around you. Although we all change, you have to learn to take control of your life and all the changes that come with it. However, you will realize that you need help along the way, because times do become difficult. You can't always do things by yourself: like the saying goes, "It takes a village to raise a child."

About three years ago, when I was just beginning the sixth grade, I went through some significant changes, both physically and mentally. After two weeks into the 2001–02 school year, and after I'd scoped the scene, I figured out that being in middle school was all about hip-hop music, name brand clothes, new shoes, and a whole lot of attitude. I was a shy, straight-A, female student who had come into this new world where acceptance, popularity, and relationships were important. I only talked to three friends, but I conversed with my teachers frequently. But that changed quickly. I figured out I wanted to roll with those who had the most fun. I began to hide my interest in my classwork, and my behavior became noticeably different. To the outside world I was loud, defiant, and disruptive—and obviously traveling with the wrong crowd.

My behavior and physical appearance were disturbing. I had been slacking on my schoolwork. Boys had become a huge part of my life, and sad to say, were more important than family or school. I talked on the phone at least three times longer than I spent on homework or reading. I gave in to just about everything. And, well, I became more social with guys. Boys can make girls do some seriously crazy things, and I wasn't a girl who could easily say no.

I had joined a gang and included myself in "jumpings." Being in a gang was like having a second family, maybe even closer than a family. The majority of the things we did, families don't do together. We rolled everywhere together, did all of our dirt together, and no matter how "hard" we might have seemed, we had each other's backs in *most* circumstances.

It took work to keep our "team" together, mainly because, though we were on the same general side, there were internal conflicts. Specifically, there were personality clashes. There were too many people trying to lead, and also, too many people going along without thinking. Others didn't want to put in their share of work, but they still wanted to be known as gang members. My team wasn't going to let that happen, so fights took place within the team.

After three or four months, I thought, "Who wants to be a part of this?" It was an unorganized, dysfunctional group of delinquents that did more bad than good. I also had a reputation now, something I had never been familiar with before. I became known as a smart aleck, "fast," and extremely aggressive, because I spent the majority of my time with boys. It was obviously not beneficial to me. So I wanted out, but I knew it would be at a terrible cost. I had to weigh out the options and make one of the most difficult choices I'd ever have to make in my life. I had to either endure the physical pain of leaving the gang, or stay and continue to plummet downhill.

I began to truly understand the speeches I'd been given before, about how I was so much more special than how I was portraying myself. You know, those "reaching your full potential" speeches and the "you're better than that" lectures that you don't really listen to. Well, eventually I listened and understood. I understood because of how I was treated by both males and females. I had been in at least five fights (one with a guy) and had more exes than four of my friends had had their entire lives.

Knowing that I had to be physically beaten in order to escape helped me figure out that the gang was truly not family—family would not do that. My blood family, they were my real family, the ones I could return to under *any* circumstance. They constantly showed persistence and care. Throughout that year, my mom delivered speech after speech and never gave up on me. Honestly, I didn't see why she was so relentless. We both knew that her words went in one ear and out the other because I was so used to her lecturing. In addition, when my father phoned (he has lived in Las Vegas since I was three), he told me how disappointed he was, but that he still loved me and hoped that I "got it together" before it was too late. At the time I didn't understand what that meant, but I did understand that I had let him down. And if there was something that I always wanted from my dad, it was his approval. Now I didn't have it, and it bothered me. But no matter how saddened he was, he was persistent, like my mother. He did show disappointment, but he also showed love.

My cousin also shared her real-life experience, having been in the exact situation herself. She told me that gangs were dangerous and extremely negative, but most importantly, she told me how they rip you from your real family and hurt all of those around you. They all affected me positively by showing me more love and determination than any gang member could have ever done. My family was extremely important to me, especially to my potential success in life.

My teachers were also very important to me. They helped me appreciate my life and literally showed me how to get around all the obstacles in my way. When my English teacher saw me with my "friends," she told me to come into her classroom. She asked me why I was with them. I told her we were placed outside the classroom because we were misbehaving, and she asked me a question that I really had no answer to: "Was your behavior your decision or was it just a ricochet?" Things were starting to make sense.

My family and teachers all came together as a team to work on my improvement. My family was there to show their love and persistence, and my teachers were there physically, seeing exactly what I was doing and pulling me out of situations. They all cared for me when I needed them most.

I had to contemplate where I was headed if I continued on the same track. I put myself through some serious stress, thinking about my final decision. I had to determine what was more important to me: a couple of minutes of pain, or the severe and long-lasting pain of my family when I was seriously injured, or (God forbid) dead. Once I narrowed it down to those two options, the answer really was plain and simple: I couldn't stay in that gang.

When I confronted the gang, they didn't believe I was serious. They thought I was joking. There were many arguments and a few yelling matches. They were surprised and obviously angry. I don't want to say that they exactly understood, but up to a certain point, they did. A couple of days went by with no problems, and then . . . they caught me by surprise.

One day after school a couple of the gang members, including my "big homie" and my best friend at the time (who was also in the gang), took me behind the bungalows and threatened me. They told me I had to fight with my best friend or get jumped by them. Once again I was faced with a difficult choice. But I didn't have much time to deliberate. So I chose to fight my friend.

Although it lasted for a of couple seconds, it seemed like an hour.

When we were both tired, we stopped, backed away, and looked at each other with an "I'm sorry" look of pity. The guys just laughed and talked about me (because honestly, I lost). I wanted to cry, but I didn't want to show them how much they had hurt me. So I walked away, head held high, and went home.

By the middle of summer 2002, I was completely turned around, changed, once again. My appearance was more acceptable, my behavior was excellent, and my grades increased dramatically. From this experience, I learned that acceptance and satisfaction start with me. Also, I came to understand that all change is not good change. Lastly and most importantly, I learned that in the worst of situations, only the support of those closest to me can provide the final push home.

SONG OF PRIDE
CANDICE MONROE

I will make it
By God's grace
I can take it
With God in first place

My family, my teachers
My church and my preachers
They are my choir
With them, I aspire

I will sing
Through the rain
And drown out
All my pain

When I fall
To a dark, low place
I will reach with my all
And stay in the race

Lifting me up is my choir
Along with them
I REJOICE
Higher and higher

I can envision
My goal is in sight
I can achieve it
By God's might

I will finish high school

And then go to college
With my goals
And my knowledge

Through all of the things
That pace through my head
With God on my team
I will push ahead

Lifting me up is my choir
Along with them
I REJOICE
Higher and higher

These are the words
That I will cry
I know this song
Will never die

My choir is my team
Forever on my side
This is
My Song of Pride!

TO BE, OR NOT TO BE?
THAT WAS THE QUESTION;
MY TROUPE WAS THE ANSWER
ALLISON HOWARD

It was blessed. It was spiritual. It was my calling. It was the day I felt pure happiness. I was complete because I owned it. It was my creation, and I wanted it to be perfect. I wanted it to have a great sound and a fresh smell. I wanted the sweet odors of the audience to fill the air. I wanted the actors to inhale those odors and exhale my handwritten lines. To further string along my happiness, I wanted my parents to hear those lines out of the performers' mouths and wonder in complete ignorance who they originated from, and for me to come into their minds, a small voice: me, it was me. Then I would have made my parents happy. They feel like it's theirs because I'm theirs. I am what they've worked so hard to perfect and now I had worked hard to perfect something of my own. 'Til this day and forever on I will never forget my first play, not only because it is one of my most memorable accomplishments, but because this passionate experience could not have expressed its sense of beauty if it were not for my team: the actors.

I stood there with my team behind the stage and I didn't give them a speech. They did not need to be told how important this day was, not just for me, but for us. We had been through so much in our quest for perfection. There were times when each of us wanted to give up. Our personalities would clash, and we would think the worst of each other. But we had to train ourselves to work together for the result we all wanted. We had to leave our selfish outlook on life behind because the reality was, we needed each other for our success. We knew our performance as a whole would define us as individuals.

The first scene was set and the actors took their positions. After saying a prayer to myself, I looked on and assisted them with their positioning. Ready, let's go. The room went pitch black, then the stage was lit. I gave the OK, but I heard no words. "Please don't do this," I thought to myself. The natural processes of breathing decided they would take a pause in the middle of my throat. I waited and waited for what seemed like hours. All of a sudden the first line was spoken, and I closed my eyes as if it were sweet music to my ears. From that point on I had nothing to worry about. It was in the hands of my team, and they were in the hands of God. All as one, we would present a form of dramatic perfection that only a team could.

I had seen many plays before and marveled at their ability to hold your attention. The audience would walk into the illuminated theater not really knowing what to expect. After the tiring experience of ticket checking and seat mix-ups, you would think their drive to be entertained would have faded, and yet they sat there with anticipation until the performance began. The way those actors spoke and moved, the way they associated with one another and reacted to each other's words and comments held you there, and you were their captive. I wanted to be responsible for other people's captivity. I felt the attention my team of actors received—this is why I encouraged their exaggeration of my words. When the audience laughed, they laughed with me, and when they were still, in deep thought, they were watching me. I felt hundreds of people staring at me, yet I stood in an empty hallway with a marked-up script in hand. I could feel it, and I loved it. I loved when the actors expressed perfect lines and when they made mistakes. Together, they caressed me and made me feel warm. The idea should have scared me, forced me to quit and run from those who needed me—the individuals—whom I needed as well. Instead, they completed me and brought my visions to life: my acting team. I stood there smiling, feeling a sense of fulfillment.

From the roaring sounds of the applause and the oh-so-lovely remarks, one would say that this play was a success. However, even if my first-born had somehow failed, it had opened the door for something even greater. This was a step to eternal happiness. It was what I wanted to do. And I needed my team of beautiful actors for the peace I wanted to feel in my chosen career. I needed their emotions, reflexes, talents, but most importantly, I needed their best, just as they did mine. We each had to put forth equal amounts of dedication and hard work while never losing sight of the union we created. We were a team, and together we needed to strive for greatness. Our purpose was to produce great entertainment, and as a troupe the outcome would be uncommon. Many teams fail because they can't seem to understand that their togetherness is what brings them victory. I thank God my team learned this sooner rather than later.

I could write a million monologues and express them to others over and over again, but the feeling wouldn't be the same. It wouldn't have the same effect on me or my audience. It's the beauty of teamwork that makes it great, and many people have yet to learn this. In my case, I will never forget it. The value of a great performance achieved by individuals connected through a team is something we all should cherish; it is an experience unlike any other.

I had just one purpose and objective: to turn fifteen and have a *Quinceañera*—a big party to celebrate my fifteenth birthday. My party preparation started early in October, a few months before my birthday. Everything had to be perfect for that day, the day I was going to stop being a child and become a woman.

It was a cold November morning. At 6:30 A.M. a persistant buzzing echoed in my ear. It was the voice of my uncle telling me softly, *"Dispiertate mija, ahora es tu gran dia"* ("Wake up, daughter of mine, today is your big day."). I got up so quickly it made my head spin.

The moment I stepped out of my room, I smelled the penetrating odor of the hairspray and flowery gel that the stylist was using on my mother's hair.

I walked into the laundry room that had been rearranged into a temporary hair salon. I was asked to sit on a hard, wooden chair in the center of this cold and damp room. The hairstylist was ready for my transformation. Makeup. This was the thing I always asked my mother for permission to wear, but the response was always the same: "You're too young." Makeup: The thing that made me look older, the thing I'd been waiting for since I was a little girl. Makeup: The thing I saw my older cousins wearing and wanted to wear myself, but they just put lip gloss on me so I would go away. But this was my day to be awarded special privileges, including getting my hair done, getting my nails manicured, and last but not least, putting on makeup!

At this point, it was time for the most important part of turning fifteen: the *Quinceañera* dress. Mine was outstanding, and creating it united my entire family. They worked together as a team, the communal goal being to escort me into adulthood. Our objectives were that the dress fit me perfectly and that the day be the first memory of my adult life. My Tia Paz was in charge of putting the dress together. She was a fundamental member of Team Elizabeth. The dress was pink, traditional for females and also my favorite color; it was simple, but beautiful. It had white flowers embroidered at the bottom—marvelous in my eyes. My cousins Alex and Maria ("Chole," we call her) and Maria's husband Victor were in charge of getting my "bling bling," because every young lady has to have some bling in her life.

Finally, I was just a few minutes away from being presented to society as a young lady. I drove to the church where everyone was waiting, and I was introduced. The scent of fresh flowers penetrated my nose and the candles gave off the irritating aroma of a burning match and hot wax. Mass seemed to pass like a shooting star. I came in as a child and left as a young lady standing tall and proud.

After mass we took pictures at the park, and everyone was there. I did the catwalk and finally it was time for the party—a party made possible by Team Elizabeth, who worked to make my fifteenth birthday unforgettable. My godparents, Alicia and Ezequiel—the main leaders of my team—hosted the party. My Tio Beto paid for the ballroom and the food.

Each individual in Team Elizabeth was responsible for a piece of my new life. When I entered the ballroom the spicy aroma of enchiladas, carnitas, and rice and beans tickled my nose. The feast, the dance, the fog machine—it all made me light-headed, bringing me up into heaven and down to earth over and over again. The flashing lights blinded me as I danced to a rapid beat. I felt the beat coursing through my veins, and my heart was beating insanely to the music. My eardrums thumped as if they were the drums in the music. I danced all night until I no longer felt fatigued. This long day had come to an end and I was now a young lady, and I had had a ball worthy of one.

After my *Quinceañera*, I sat on my porch and I thought about all the hard work that it had taken to make this day so special for me. I saw how my family members had banded together to make my childhood dream come true.

Who could have thought that *Halo 2* and a subscription to Xbox Live would've brought seven distinct people together?

Alejandro Barba
AKA Alex, twenty-one years old
Now . . .
The sound of the phone ringing brought me to my feet. I pushed aside our half-broken computer chair and ran to pick up the phone before the answering machine beat me to it.

It was Alex.

Alex is a very shy individual with an open heart. When he first met us, the "hey-lets-go-to-Cheli's-house-uninvited" crew, he wasn't in such a hot spot. He was going through some emotional problems. Alex is a twenty-year-old college student with a lot of potential, but he has no idea what he wants to do for the rest of his life. When he hangs out with us, all of his troubles just go away. And you know what? It's the same for the rest of the crew.

I knew it was Friday, and I knew the reason behind his phone call before I even picked up the phone. He asked me the same question he asks every single Friday: "Hey Cheli, whatcha doin'?"

Then . . .
I remember being at my cousin Peter's birthday party. I was watching all of the little ones run around, watching them play in a little play-house. My aunt was serving nachos and my uncles were drinking the night away. Family gatherings are always so beautiful. I was letting the feeling take me in—that is, until my mother broke my trance.

"*¡Ven Cheli! ¡Déjame presentarte a tu primo Alex! ¡Ven!*" she yelled out from across the yard.

I turned around full of embarrassment, checking if anyone had noticed. 'Course they did! Everyone recognizes my mother's howls—they're like shrieking roosters! I quietly scurried over to where my mom and Alex were standing.

"¡Ya sé amá! He's my second cousin, I know!" I looked at him, smiled, nodded, and walked over to, as they say, properly introduce myself.

"Hey, I'm Cheli. Looks like you're stuck with me now, sucker." He laughed and replied, "It can't be that bad."

The feeling I had that day could not be described by words. Today, it cannot be described at all.

Erika C. Alvarez
AKA Errka, nineten years old
Now . . .

"*One new message.*" "Cheliiiiiiiiiii! Cheeeeeeeeeeeeliiiii! Pick up the phone! Ugh. I know you're right there listening to this message right now! Damn it . . . Well, Alex is on his way. I'm going to go and get ready. I'll see you in a bit. *Seven thirty-six P.M. BEEP.*"

I recognized the voice and smiled. It was my cousin, my other half, my best friend, and my partner in crime, Erika.

Erika isn't all that great at Halo. But she doesn't come over to play. She comes over because it just feels right. I can honestly say that it's not the environment that makes us feel like it's home; it's the people you love and love you that make it feel like it's home.

Love in this cold world can take you anywhere.

Then . . .

Thanksgiving last year, my dad parked the car right in front of my grandmother's house in Marina del Rey. I stepped out of the car and heard some noises coming from the lawn across the street. It was my cousins, Erika, Jeanette, and Wendy. All are gorgeous, but Erika stood out above the rest (well, after all, she is about 5'7"). I walked over and said "Happy Thanksgiving" to all of them and handed Erika a card I made especially for her. The cover had a picture of the both of us picking each other's noses. I simply smiled, turned around, and walked into the house to greet the rest of the caring, loving, beautiful, sometimes obnoxious members of the Alvarez family—yep, all sixty of them. She walked in after me and rushed to stand directly in front of me. She stared down at me with those brown puppy eyes and asked me curiously, "You only made me one?" I laughed.

Jose Serrano Jr.
AKA Josey, sixteen years old
Now . . .

I delete Erika's message and turn on my computer. I sit down on my half-broken computer chair and pull myself forward to face the computer screen. I sign onto IM. I see "TagHimIn360" on and right away I instant-message him.

"Dorkster88: Joseyyyyy!"

Then...

"Jeez! That's so stupid!"

I stormed out of the kitchen with tears in my eyes. I had just gotten into a huge argument with my mom. I wanted to get out of there but I had nowhere to go.

I ran outside. I knew Alex was coming over, so I figured I'd wait and calm down a little bit. I sat on the sidewalk with my back against our concrete gate. My mind kept reenacting the horrible fight scene in the kitchen with my mother. I just had all of my anger and sorrow bottled up inside and I let it all out on my mom. I needed to escape. A silver Toyota RAV-4 passed by and I recognized it. Right after the car parked, Alex got out and walked over to me with his head down and with both his hands in his pockets. I got up, wiped my salty tears, and he hugged me.

"Where's Jose?" I asked, trying to clean my *mocos* with the back of my hand.

"He's in the car. I didn't know if you wanted him to see you crying. What happened? "He asked worried, "Are you okay?"

"Yeah, I'm fine. It's just my mom."

"Well, what's going on? What's bothering you so much?" I think he realized I wanted to avoid the topic.

"Well, just—a lot of things. Like school, the ex, parents, the future, me above all. It's just a lot to take in at once."

"You'll be all right."

And from that moment on I was fine. It just took four simple words for me to realize that.

I walked off toward the car. Jose got out, and boy was he tall, almost a six-footer. I sniffed in my boogers and said, "Hey."

Alex introduced us. "Josey, meet your cousin Cheli. Cheli, meet Josey."

We walked inside. All of my worries were suddenly gone. The fight scene with my mother was forgotten. I didn't care about anything. It was just me, Josey, and Alex. I was at ease.

Alex greeted my parents and my brother while I introduced Josey to them.

"Oh! *¡Eres el hijo de Alicia!*" said my mom, again with the voice of shrieking roosters. Josey was so shy that you couldn't help but laugh. Our journey together began with a simple gesture: I offered Josey an Oreo cookie.

Josey doesn't really like going to the high school he's attending. His high school is known for race riots, deaths, gangs, violence, and drugs. When he comes over, we help him get away from the real world, get away from anything. It's like we have to talk or it's just a missing part in our daily lives. I can talk about anything with Josey. Imagine if Alex had never introduced us? Where would I be without his infinite wisdom?

Jeanette Alvarez
AKA Janet, twelve years old
Now . . .
"Dorkster88: So Josey, you ready yet? The hair looking OK?"
"TagHimIn360: Alex said he's on his way, and I just finished doing my hair."
"Dorkster88: Haha! You and your obsession with that hair."
Some people have a shoe fetish. Some people have a clothes fetish. Josey, well, just isn't like those people. His obsession is with his hair.
"TagHimIn360: Alex is here. I'll see you later."
"Dorkster88: M'kay."
I was about to sign off when "BriteLiteWonder92" instant-messaged me.
"BriteLiteWonder92: Heyyyy! I think Jessica is taking us to your house.
"Dorkster88: Haha. Oh jeez! Jeanette, have you realized this always happens? Alex or your brother are always calling people up and inviting them over to my house. It's hilarious, but I love it."
"BriteLiteWonder92: Haha, yeah, I know. But Peter is dumb, he invites himself everywhere."
"Dorkster88: You know, you guys should be called the 'Hey-let's-go-to-Cheli's-house-uninvited' crew."
"BriteLiteWonder92: Haha. Shut up, before I beat you with a pillow again."
Then . . .
"Jeanette! No, Jeanette! C'mon, don't do it! JEANETTE!"
Before I knew it I was on the floor. Again. I got pushed off of my own bed and flew onto that smelly carpet that never gets vacuumed.

"I win!" Jeanette started bouncing up and down on my bed. It was war.

"Rematch!" I yelled, trying to lift myself up off the floor.

"Fine," said Jeanette, too sure of herself.

I got up off the floor and began walking over to my bed. She reached over and grabbed the biggest pillow of them all, and I realized it was my doom. She had gotten to it before I even had a chance to.

War had again begun.

I grabbed the closest pillow to me, and I swung.

I missed. This was her chance to get me.

She missed, and she let loose her only source of protection. It was now my revenge.

I reach for the weapon she had let go of. The pillow hits her straight in the gut. She falls over onto her side holding her stomach while I tower over her. She just can't stop laughing. Tears of joy escape my eyes. Before I know it, I have joined her: I can't stop laughing myself.

It often seems to me that Jeanette feels more at home here in my house than in her own. She's a mature girl, smack in the middle of her sisters and brother. Her sister is eighteen, her brother Peter is sixteen, and her little sister is seven. She constantly fights with her sister, and she never has anyone to talk to. That's where the crew comes in. We come to the rescue and help her escape.

Francisco Alvarez Jr.
AKA Paco, fifteen years old
Now . . .

I say my good-byes over the Internet and log off IM.

I walk into the living room where my brother Paco is playing the guitar. He stops and looks at me with a confused look to try to throw me off guard. It doesn't work, so it makes it even funnier, and we both start to laugh.

"Ha ha, 'tard. What time are they coming?" Paco asks resuming his strum on the guitar.

"Uh ... around seven or eight tonight. Why?"

"Because I want to play with Alex. Plus, I miss Josey. C'mon now, what kind of a question is that?"

I just laughed. He can't ever live without his Josey and Alex. Hell, he can't live without me! We go together like green tea and a spoonful of honey. That's the honest truth.

I find it funny how my parents can complain and complain about how my fifteen-year-old brother is so secluded when they don't even take the time to try to get to know him. Long ago I stopped trying to figure out what my brother was all about. He and I broke down a barrier the day we accepted each other. We never fight. We just sit. And we enjoy the company. We don't have to tell each other what's on our minds, 'cause we just know. And we have a perfect understanding. I guess that's what living our whole lives together has done for us.

Then . . .

I came home from school on a Tuesday dreading my every step—I knew it was the day that report cards were going to screw me over. I was very disappointed because I knew I hadn't applied myself to do the best I could. One year ago today I was a sophomore at Ánimo Inglewood, a 3.0 GPA student now with a 1.8 average. I walked into the house my parents had bought six years ago and sat myself down on the couch in the living room.

I sighed.

My brother walked in a few minutes later and rummaged through the mail looking for his report card. He found mine instead, grinned, and literally threw it at me. I was feeling too blue to laugh. I opened it up and looked down upon my shame. I received the grades I had deserved. I chucked them aside.

"Well," my brother asked, "what did you get?"

"D, B, D, C, C, D," I replied.

"Damn, Cheli . . ." He shook his head in disbelief.

"What, man?" I gave him the wrong tone. I wasn't in the mood.

"You're graduating in a year and a half. What're you doing?"

I expected this from my parents, but from him? Nuh-uh. This was all new to me.

"I know I'm graduating in a year and a half. Don't give me this right now, all right?"

"Don't be stupid. You need to step it up, man. These are the years that count," he said. "Don't mess it up for yourself just because you were too lazy." He gave me a look that said a thousand crucial words.

"I know, man, I know. I'm going to do better. I will." I let out a long sigh. "You better man. Don't mess it up for yourself." He walked away into the kitchen and vanished for the rest of the day.

My parents lectured me a while that night but I wasn't paying attention; I was too busy telling myself that I was a horrible role model for my brother. I disappointed him that night. I'm the only one in the house that he looks up to, and I couldn't help but think that I'd just messed that up.

I apologized to my brother later on that night and promised I was going to start doing better. And I am—I raised my GPA. I concentrated and put more effort into school because of him. He's the only one I ever listen to. At this point in my life I don't turn to my parents for moral support. I turn to the "Hey-lets-go-to-Cheli's-house-uninvited" crew. They're the ones that keep me going. And my brother is just one of the few that keep me alive.

Pedro Alvarez Jr.

AKA Peter, sixteen years old

Now . . .

I left my brother to his guitar-playing when the phone began to ring.

"Hello?"

"Cheli!"

It was Peter.

"Yo." I love saying that word.

"Want me to bring the Plain White Ts CD?"

"Oh yeahhh! Thanks for reminding me. I forgot to tell Jeanette to tell you."

"Yeah. Well, I'll see you tonight."

"OK, later gator." I was just about to hang up the phone.

"Wait. . ." he said.

"Yeah?"

"Thanks for last night."

"Ha ha, you are very welcome, sir."

"Alright, bye."

"Bye."

There are a lot of things I love about Peter, but I love his honesty the most.

Then . . .

We were all at my cousin Michael's house for a birthday party. I can't remember whose birthday it was, but there were nachos. I grabbed what happened to be my third plate of nachos and sat on a really uncomfortable couch that was in the garage. Halfway through my plate, Peter came and joined me on the couch. It's not that he made it visible that something was troubling him, but I felt that something was.

I wasn't sure if he'd share what was bothering him with me, but I had to give it a try.

"Peter . . . you alright?"

"Huh?" He looked at me puzzled. "Oh, yeah. Well, wait. No . . ."

"Well?" I tried waiting politely, but I'm not that patient, ya know. "Alright, you don't have to tell me. It's OK."

I didn't mean it though. I really wanted to know what was bothering him. I just went back to my nachos.

"Drugs." He was talking to the floor.

I froze. If there's anything I hate most in the world, it's drugs. I see no point to them. I didn't know what to say. I mostly wanted to hit him, but I don't hit very hard, so I decided to say something instead.

"What *about* drugs? They're bad for you, you know."

Duh. I'm a true idiot sometimes.

"My friends do them."

Oh boy. Peer pressure is the worst kind of pressure anyone can be under. Teenagers are just plain mean.

"Oh . . ." Awkward silence. He just seemed lost, so I decided to break it.

"Listen. I'm not your mom, I'm not your dad. I'm not going to tell you what's wrong from right because you're old enough to make those decisions yourself." I stopped and took in a deep breath. I looked him straight in the eye. "I love you, and you know how I feel about them, but it's your life and they're your decisions to make. And I'm not going to sit here and tell you not to do them. Look, I'm not going to think less of you whether you decide to try them out or not."

He was still looking at the floor. "Thanks, Cheli." He finally looked up at me. "Anytime."

He seemed relieved. Peter doesn't go out much with the people he hangs out with because they don't have the same interests. He seems to be moving towards another different, better crowd, but it's really hard for him. He loves it when the "crew" gets together because we make him laugh and forget about the problems he has, and he always has a good time. He never used to really talk, but that's changed. His life has changed and he's taking another path. I can definitely say the same thing about the rest of us.

Now, Today, and Forever . . .

It's almost seven o'clock and I'm growing very hungry. Usually I'd call Alex and ask him how many pizzas I should order; it's usually four or five medium pepperoni pizzas with gasless coke, from the garage, which Alex seems to love. It's usually OJ (hold the pulp) for the rest of us. I figured I should call him because my stomach just wouldn't give it a rest, and I couldn't take it any longer.

"Alex! Pizza!"

"Ha ha, hold on. Let me ask the rest of them."

I can hear all the noise coming from the other end of the line. I heard Jeanette.

"Yeah, yeah. Five mediums."

"All right. Where are you guys?"

"Right outside! Open the gate."

I hung up the phone and decided I didn't want to open the gate. I'd rather see them jump it.

I heard commotion along with Jeanette banging on the front door. I opened it up and Jeanette was laughing and couldn't stop. Peter, Alex, and Erika were laughing too! The only one who wasn't really laughing was Josey. He was just bickering with Alex, telling him to shut up.

"Whatever, all right? Where's the pizza?" Josey can eat like a starving stray dog. "Where's your money? Wait, let me just collect everyone's. *Andale*, pay over," I said, sticking my hand out.

I collected everyone's money and set it on the table so that it could be easier to get ahold of when the pizza guy came.

I got up to turn on the Xbox and to grab a seat on the floor next to Josey and Alex. Josey, Alex, Paco, and I were the only ones playing at the time because Peter was learning some new songs on the guitar and Erika and Jeanette were watching movies.

After a few rounds of Team Training, we decided we wanted to try some new things out. Since we're so bad at working together as a team, we decided to create a game consisting of my brother and me on one team and Alex and Josey on another team. We wanted to find new and easier ways to play "Multi-Capture the Flag" on a map called "Burial Mounds." Alex got ahold of our flag and was running towards his base. Josey was staring at the TV screen without blinking, saying repetitively, "Gimme my flag, foo', gimme my flag, foo'. . ." while chasing behind Alex. Josey began shooting Alex, his own teammate, still saying "Gimme my flag, foo'." We all started laughing because we couldn't understand why he was shooting his own teammate if they were about to score. Finally Josey kills Alex, grabs ahold of the flag, and runs.

Alex and Josey quit for awhile. Actually, we all quit for awhile. We all just sat like a lazy bunch on the couch and just started talking about all the good times we've had. From Josey's "Gimme my flag, foo," to all of us chasing after Jeanette at a bonfire because she wanted to go swimming in the beach at 10 P.M., to Erika throwing her cell phone at my wall because she figured it was broken anyway (the dent is still there), to Paco's lame jokes that all begin with "So this fat guy walks into the bar and he says—'Hi! I'm fat!','' to Alex's pizza swimming in ranch dressing, to my power naps that last more than twenty minutes, to Peter jumping up in the air and clicking his heels together . . . all in all, in the end, it brings all of us back to my house, in the living room, all seven of us, together. Now, today, and forever.

The 'Hey-let's-go-to-Cheli's-house-uninvited' Crew

I started off this biographical story believing that teamwork consisted of a group of people who have a similar goal and do everything and anything in their power to accomplish something. Always.

Wrong.

Going to 826LA and getting professional help with my story made me realize that that's not what it's all about. I wanted to write about the crew the day I knew I was in this writing thing all the way; the only problem was that I didn't know how to incorporate "teamwork" because my definition of it was all screwed up.

People often say that family will be with you until the end—after all, they're family, right? They're stuck with you forever and sometimes only because you're related by blood. *MY* family consists of unique individuals who can turn this world upside down and fix it in less than a day because of their faith, love, and support. *MY* family is something very valuable and precious. *MY* family didn't come out of the same mother and doesn't live under the same roof I do (well . . . except for my brother Paco). *MY* family can serve your family at "Halo" any day. *MY* family is the best family anyone can ever ask for.

My name is Araceli "Cheli" Alvarez, and I'm proud to say that Alex, Errka, Josey, Jeanette, Paco, and Peter are *MY* family.

THE RHYTHM OF THE BROTHERHOOD
ELVIN S. HOYT II

Unity, the Brotherhood

Some people say they don't need it
They say I'm straight, I'm cool, it's all good

But the fact of the matter is that they need it
Whether they like it or not

Especially coming where I come from
Where without it you could get popped

I can testify, especially me
Being a young black man

In our society that's one strike
Being dark-skinned or even having a tan

Without the brotherhood, I don't know where
Our black nation will stand

Probably still segregated, blacks can't even walk around town
Or the white man still trying to keep us young brothers down

Because of unity, now we have black
Athletes, actors, and political figures

Civil rights got OGs counseling in community centers
Instead of pulling triggas

Because of that we can be viewed as something positive
Not just viewed as n****s

So before people criticize us, they start to think twice
Now blacks have people in the government like Maxine Waters
and Condoleezza Rice

The brotherhood has put blacks together in a strong band
If Malcolm X and Martin Luther King Jr. were here, they
would understand

Malcolm X led many movements, Dr. King has his own parade
They're probably looking down from heaven smiling at the
changes they made

But one day the ignorant ones will see
That the brotherhood is not something you ignore

IT IS REALITY

Before you know it, without unity, you'll be another wino on the street
Begging for a dollar or trying to get something to eat

So if you don't want to be did dirty
And left in the cold like ice, you better get your mind right

UNITY, THE BROTHERHOOD

It's something you need in your life

Thursday Morning, As the Sun Ascended

Conor awoke with my eyes on him. I had spent the night in his closet watching as he slept. What he dreamt, who could truly know? I had been stalking him since the day before. I would haunt his every step like a loyal hound at the foot of his master. He awoke that November morning at 7:20 A.M. for his 7:30 A.M. departure. This was typical for his type. You know the type: those who are never on time, seldom prepared, never secure about anything in life. Slowly, he got up. He removed his shirt, and it landed upon the mountains and peaks of clothes that blanketed his floor. Then he opened his closet door. I hurtled myself into a corner so I could not be seen. He inspected his clothes, an array of black. Who was the boy trying to kid? He threw on a shirt, XXL. He was a rather big boy. While he was still getting dressed, he heard the repetitive screech that came from the car. As he persisted, he did not even bother with his reflection. It wouldn't matter after this day anyway, he thought.

Wednesday Afternoon, The Day Before

Conor was in biology class. The teacher, Mr. Graves, never took a genuine liking to him. He believed that Conor had too much natural ability to let decay because of something as naive as a lack of motivation. Because of this, they resented each other. As Mr. Graves was in the front of the class reviewing for an upcoming exam, I could see Conor wandering thoughtlessly within his head. He had made up his mind. He no longer had any need for education, so he just sat there humming to himself. He was in the back of the class at the last table in the very corner. Three other people sat with him at this table, but he was alone. As his mindless non-thoughts continued, he realized he was deserted in this place. Sixteen years of his life had passed him by, and he had accomplished nothing to show for it. So at that moment he decided that he was no longer going to be a student of conformity. He was going to create his own path. In truth, Conor knew nothing of what he spoke. Ignorance truly is bliss.

Confrontation #1, His Aunt and the White Van

Conor marched toward the 1992 white Astro van. It retained so many memories. His right hand, which was as colorless as a bloodless body, clenched the handle and jerked the door back. The door lunged. He stepped into the van. Once he was seated and the door was securely sealed, the motor of the van started up. The trembling seats shook him aside for a second, and as the van exited the driveway, he received the question he was awaiting but at the same moment dreading.

"Why aren't you dressed in your uniform?" asked his aunt.

"I'm only going to school today because I need to check out."

"Does your mom know?"

"Yeah."

You could immediately sense the emptiness of words unsaid and feelings abandoned. As his aunt began to drive, she glared at the immortal road, which was paved in agony. His cousin, who was two years younger than he, sat beside her in the front seat. Even at her age, she was aware of the brutal honesty of life. Her silence spoke of how despondent and companionless life is. How the strong feed off the weak and the weak feed off themselves.

As he stepped away from the white vehicle, which seemed to be degenerating from the inside because of its unkemptness, he was not only abandoning the van but his family as well. He walked, his pace so nonchalant, full of pride and self-esteem. In an instant of a stare, knowledge vanished.

Confrontation #2, The Friend Who Once Was

As soon as he set foot on the thronged patio, the populace of souls evaporated, leaving only one. She stared into his eyes with concern and wonder.

"I wasn't expecting to see you today."

"I had to show up for a study session."

"So why aren't you in uniform?" she wondered.

"I'm leaving school today."

"You can't just leave the school!" she shrilled.

"Sure I can, that's what I'm here for. I'm just going to sign out and be gone."

"If you leave I'm going to cry."

"Jenn, I'm sorry but I have to go. I'll call you later. OK?"

"You better not leave! Just give it some time."

"I have. Trust me. I've made up my mind. I don't need your advice." He spoke with self-assurance and with little care for any emotion that overcame her.

From behind the stairs where I stood watching him, I noticed a look of bewilderment hit his entire body. His eyes began to lose concentration and his footing stumbled. He began to doubt if his decision was the correct one. But then he injected himself with another dose of ignorance and pride.

The Voice of Intimidation, Tyson

Right after he began walking, a security guard, Mr. Tyson, called him. The guard's stern voice and stare penetrated every inch of his body.

Conor heard the identical question for the fourth time that day.

"Why aren't you in uniform?" he asked.

"I'm leaving the school."

"Go straight to the office" Mr. Tyson said. "You can't be down here. I don't want to see you talking to anyone else."

The Screech of Regulation and Irritation

The security guard made him realize something: he realized that he was no longer a part of this school. He did not want to be associated with the school and the school wanted nothing with him. He was no longer a student. In the span of a few minutes, he became a drifter, a vagrant, an outcast.

He proceeded to the office without hesitation. Every person in viewing distance began to scrutinize him, but he just continued to walk.

Once Conor reached the office he saw that Mrs. Howard, the school's counselor was waiting for him. Tyson had called ahead and warned her about Conor's situation.

"What's up?" she asked.

"I'm here to check out."

"You can't do that. You need a parent to do that."

"Fine. I'll just come back tomorrow or something."

"We can't let you go. Once you get dropped off at school, you're in our custody. We are responsible for you now."

At this point, to him, each of her words was more irritating than the next.

"Fine, just call my aunt and have her pick me up. I'll wait around here."

His First Hello

After storming out of the office, he knocked on the door of his former teacher. She had done so much for him, so much that words could not even put it into perspective. She was the only person to whom he could turn. Mrs. Groban opened her door, then shut it right behind him.

"What's up? Why aren't you in class? Why aren't you in uniform?"

He paused as if to gather the courage to admit it. "I'm leaving the school."

"Oh my God! Why?" Her high-pitched voice was hushed with discreet concern.

"I don't really know. Just don't feel like I belong to this place anymore."

The classroom was dimly lit by the minuscule amount of sunlight coming through the three windows with the black trim. The blinds were half open, and trees partially covered the windows.

The empty classroom seemed secluded and unattended. Mrs. Groban continued: "Promise me you're not going to drop out of school."

He gave a nervous smile, like someone who is trying to lie but cannot keep a steady face.

"You can take a break from school, but you have to promise me that you're going to graduate."

Her eyes began to leak.

"I need to see you succeed. Other people aren't as fortunate as you. I know people who try and try, but still do not understand the things you do. You have a gift, and you shouldn't let it go to waste."

Her tears began to fall into him, and he struggled to maintain himself. His pride and ego would not allow him to admit that he had made a wrong decision. She moved in for a hug, but he could not bring himself to hug her back. He could not gather himself to show that he was delicate, that he was a sensitive soul, that he was scared of his choice, scared of what would become of him. He had not only abandoned his family and friends, but now he had abandoned himself.

The Realization

I watched him through all this and much more. I knew what he was thinking, I knew what he was feeling, I knew everything. I knew him so well because he is me. I was truly the eye of regret. I had abandoned everyone and everything. But when you refuse help from others and won't help yourself, you can only get so far.

In my life I've seen many relationships that never worked: for example, my parents. My parents are my parents—no one can change that, but sometimes I wish I could. While growing up, I always saw the fights they had and I remember getting scared and feeling like I was in the middle of it all. My parents never thought of the consequences that these constant arguments would bring.

Now I realize that not all relationships are like that, for example, my boyfriend and I. We've discovered a team within us. We are together through good and bad, you know? It's like, if I fall, he's there to pick me up and be by my side. I would do the same thing for him. A couple not only must be there physically, but mentally as well. We can be together in our thoughts and always know there's no limit to how close we can become.

Looking back, I thought that this day would be like any other day: going to school, hanging out with my friends, going to class, and going home. But this day wasn't the same as the other boring days. As usual, I was in class. It was fourth period, algebra class. Ms. Simmons teaches this class, and my friend, Martha sits next to me. Behind Martha, was the guy of my dreams. Back then we were "close" friends—how disappointing.

We always passed notes, never on regular paper but on Post-Its. On this day he whispered in his firm, deep voice, "Let me see your Post-Its." Without making eye contact, smiling inside, I reached inside my backpack and handed him an entire Post- It pad. This is where I wrote flirtatious nothings on half of the pad. I thought we were going to have a normal conversation about "What We Did," and "What Are You Doing," but today was a whole new set of notes.

Out of nowhere he mentioned his ex-girlfriend and wrote about how he was sad, but mostly doing OK. I flipped to what seemed like the forty-fifth note when suddenly he asked me why I liked him. *What! How did he know?* He then told me that a couple of days ago his ex-girlfriend told him she heard *rumors* that I liked him. I guess the *rumors* were started because we were "close" friends and we were always together. I guess people thought we were going out, but they didn't bother to ask us.

Totally shocked about what had just happened, I took the notes home and tried to figure out my next move. When I got home I thought to myself, *What am I going to do? What am I going to say? What is he going to think of me?* I tried to find different ways I could escape this situation, but I found no exit. I realized, *I'll tell him the truth.* Then that idea disappeared into thin air, because I could never do that. I started to think of the consequences there would be if I told him the truth. I didn't want to risk it. I didn't want him to reject me, and especially, I didn't want to ruin our friendship. For that reason, I decided to keep my mouth shut.

After school I was sitting by the computer, writing in my diary about what happened that day. With the TV, radio, and my brother and sister screaming, it was very distracting. Somehow I got back on track. Suddenly, I jumped out of my seat when the phone rang. It was him with the big question. The big question was, "Do you like me as more than a friend?" I really didn't want to ruin our friendship, so I explained that it couldn't be more because we were always there when we needed help, and nothing would ever be the same if our friendship became a relationship. He agreed, but I don't think either of us believed it.

Minutes later I said, "Well, I like you because of who you are." He said, "I'm who I am because of you. You are always there for me." Hearing those words, tears filled my eyes, and I couldn't swallow.

He then asked, "Do you like anyone else?"

I said honestly, "I only like you."

Later he asked, "So, do you want me to ask you out?"

Feeling that this was a pity ask-out, I said, "I don't want you to ask me out if you feel I'm forcing you to."

He blurted out, "No one is forcing me! I want to go out with you, but I fear you'll cheat or leave me!"

That's ridiculous! I liked him so much that I wouldn't do that! I told him not to fear this because I would always be there when he needed me, no matter what! I finally said yes, I'd go out with him, which made me feel happy because I didn't have to lie to him anymore. Now that we're together, I have the chance to say "I love you," and I can show my love by being by his side and never pushing this love aside.

As I look back, I believed that just because I saw relationships go bad, then I would have a bad one too. My parents' relationship is based on fights and a lack of love. Is that teamwork? NO! So I ask myself, *Am I part of a team?* Yes, I am. He and I do a lot of things together: we go to the movies together, we hang out together, and we talk on the phone every day. When he doesn't call me, it breaks my heart because I want to hear his voice and just talk. We also help each other out. When he's sometimes depressed, I'm always there to help him through that phase. We are together. We are a team.

There are different types of relationships—there are ones like my parents have, and on the other hand, there is ours. As long as we're together, working as a team, that's what truly matters.

THE BRIGHTEST COLOR
ROCIO SAMUEL-GAMA

"Kristen was shot. Three bullets to the chest and one to the leg."

These are the words I heard just before hanging up my cell phone.

It was a dark, gray night and I was at my grandma's house with my friends Marissa, Amy, and my cousins Jessica and Leslie. We were sitting around talking, eating, and drinking hot chocolate with marshmallows.

Around ten o'clock at night my cell phone started playing the "Oops, I Did it Again" song. I thought it was probably one of my friends calling to ask what we were doing, but she didn't call for that reason . . . she called to say those awful words.

We all rushed to the car and drove for the longest thirty minutes of my life. As my cousin Leslie drove, everyone was silent, shocked, and frightened. We finally arrived at the spot in Gardena where the shooting had occurred.

Aside from just one street lamp, the night was pitch black. There were many trees around the large grass field, where a blood puddle surrounded Kristen's body. The friend who had called earlier ran up to me; Marissa and Jessica ran to her body. I was stunned and confused. Everything was spinning out of control. An ambulance rushed to the park, and nosy people came out of their homes.

As the paramedics took the body away, we cried, shoulder to shoulder. Kristen was dead, and I didn't want to believe it. She had just been at my house the other day. No, this did not just happen.

Our parents arrived, worried, and they asked my cousin Leslie what had just happened. When I left, I was relieved that I didn't have to stand in the park any longer.

During the ride home, I was sullen. I wanted to tell the people who had taken my best friend's life how much I hated them. I wanted to yell and scream at them because they killed an innocent person—she had never hurt anyone.

When I got home I went straight to my room and slammed my door. I asked myself "Why her?" and "What the hell was she thinking?"

My mom looked for words to comfort me. In my head I told myself, "She doesn't understand—I just want to be alone." I said, "Mom, you might have lost a friend too, but this is different, because I just lost a sister."

"I'm sorry for your loss," she said, and then she left the room.

Kristen and I had grown up together. We had known each other since the second grade, and since then nobody could come between us. We played on the same basketball team along with our friends. She knew everything about me, and I knew everything about her.

The day of the memorial service I dressed in a black skirt and a black see-through blouse with a yellow shirt underneath. I put on the yellow hoop earrings Kristen had given me the year before for my birthday. She always liked bright colors, but yellow was her favorite: she liked yellow because she figured since the sun was the brightest star, then yellow would be the brightest color.

Later, my basketball friends entered my room one by one. They were each wearing yellow.

No one spoke. We just sat there and cried, hugging each other, keeping ourselves together, and knowing how we each felt.

When my friends got up to leave for the service, I just sat there on my bed; I didn't want to go. Attending the service would be like accepting that she was really gone.

"Are you coming?" Amy asked.

"No."

"Why not?" Marissa demanded.

"Because I don't want to. I want to be by myself."

"Too bad." Amy said. "You're going whether you want to or not."

They dragged me along to the memorial service at the mortuary. Everyone was afraid of what we would see and feel.

When we entered the chapel, it smelled strongly of a mixture of cologne and perfume. It was quiet except for Kristen's mother, Patty, who was sobbing by the coffin; Kristen's older siblings were hugging and comforting her.

I told Patty I loved her, and I gave her a hug. My friends followed and cried along with her. I stared at her with emptiness and noticed that everyone around me was crying—but I couldn't.

As more people arrived and grieved, I remembered a time not so long ago. *Kristen and some friends and I had been playing basketball at another friend's house. It started to rain but we continued playing. The next thing I knew, I was in an ambulance with Kristen on the way to the hospital. I was crying because the doctors said she had pneumonia and weren't sure if she would make it. Kristen told me: "Don't cry for me; I don't like it when people cry. Just be strong, and I will always be your best friend."*

When I came back to reality, I knew she was sending me a message: that although she was dead, she would still have my back, and she was in a better place. I left the memorial service with my friends feeling as if I were on a cloud, knowing that she would never abandon me.

At home I took out pictures of the two of us. I fell asleep with her presence in my dreams, and I knew everything would be OK.

The next day was The Day—the day my best friend would be buried six feet underground.

My friends and I arrived at the cemetery in a fresh-smelling, quiet limousine. Mostly older women and a few young women were seated in chairs, the men were standing around. The priest arrived in the second limousine with Kristen's family.

The funeral went like any other. Kristen was buried, and people were crying.

We left, holding tightly to her memory.

Kristen was someone who was loyal and caring. She had always been there to support me and take my side. My best friend was understanding and always made the right choice. My best friend was there for me morning, day, and night. My best friend was the one who stood out and tried her best.

As the weeks went by, my friends and I kept ourselves distracted. When people at school asked about Kristen, we said "We don't want to talk about it," and walked away.

Three weeks after her death, before a big basketball game we practiced hard all afternoon. That night, at the game, the coach put me and four of my best friends on the court. We played hard, as one great team, united. With two minutes left, down by one point, the coach called time-out. We gathered and decided on a play that Kristen had come up with awhile back. The referee blew the whistle and it was our ball.

Marissa took out the ball and passed it to Amy. Amy dribbled to the top of the key and passed it to Janet. Janet passed it to me, and I passed it to Nancy. There were two seconds left. Nancy took two steps, shot the ball, and *swish*. We won the game!

We had suffered a tragic event, and if it weren't for all of us sticking together, I know I would have fallen apart. I also know that Kristen will always be there for me spiritually.

1. I eat.
2. I wash my dish.
3. I go to my room and do my homework.
4. Then I have a little time to talk on the phone.

Ariana

My name is Ariana Acevedo. I am almost sixteen years old. I attend Ánimo Inglewood Charter High School; I really like it. My home life is not what some people expect for a teenager. When I go home, it's almost like I am the adult. I have to take care of business. The minute I step in, it's, "Hurry up and eat so you can go do something." This is what my mother says every time I walk in the house. I have to baby-sit my little sister Jocelyne and help her do her homework.

Tough Times

I go to sleep at eleven or twelve each night. When I wake up, I do not see my father—he has two jobs. I miss his love, our time to talk, and even having him ordering me to do things around the house. I also miss my mother. When I get home from school, I only see her for about three hours. Then she leaves for work and comes back when I am getting ready for bed. On weekends, I am so exhausted. This is the time when I want to go out and have a little fun—I want to be with my friends. I often feel that I don't have anyone to talk to, or anyone who truly cares about me. I have so much love stored in my heart for the perfect someone in my life yet nobody to share it with.

Chris

I met him at a party and we started to talk. He let me escape from everything that was going on in my life. I felt so much better being around him. When I would see him, I would feel loved. Later, he lost interest because my mom did not want me to go out with him. I liked him a lot.

Jonathan

It took about three months to recover from the relationship with Chris. Then one day while I was at my friend Arlyn's house, I met her cousin Jonathan. When I first met him, I didn't think he was the type of guy I was into because we had such different interests. The days would pass, and Jonathan would try "to get with me." I never wanted him. He would bother me, and I did not like that. Yet he stayed interested in me for months.

The Connection

At some point, without knowing why, I started feeling close to Jonathan. When we were left alone, I felt butterflies in my stomach. I had never felt that way. These feelings were so important to me. I was afraid they might go away. I felt like I was on the clouds, waiting for someone to tell me it was all a lie.

The day before the Fourth of July, I went to my friend Arlyn's house for a barbeque, and Jonathan was there. We spent the day together and everything was great. We kissed many times, and it felt like it was a wonderful dream. We were both so relaxed. I was wishing the day would never end. Before I left, we kissed one last time. When I went home, I could not stop thinking about Jonathan. I had him in my dreams and on my mind. When I woke up in the morning, he was still there. He was everything I could ever want. I felt the love connection between us. I did not feel alone.

Later, I realized there were many consequences to this relationship. I think that I was too into Jonathan. I forgot about Andre, my very best friend in the whole world—I've known him since I was in the fourth grade, but I did not speak to him all summer. My grades in school dropped dramatically; I stopped taking care of my sister and helping her with her homework. I put Jonathan first in my life over anything else. I was so disappointed in myself.

Jonathan came to my *Quinceañera*, but after that he started acting like he did not want to talk to me. I felt the emptiness. When I saw him, he would ignore me. I felt lonely. I was desperate to talk or be with someone.

Andre

I still had my best friend Andre. Three months passed by, and Andre and I became close. I started to realize that he was all I wanted in a guy: he liked everything about me, we could talk about anything. It was something special. We do not have to do anything to be happy. We can be together all day and not get bored. Sometimes we just talk. This relationship was really meant to be.

Lessons in Love

I have learned from all of these relationships. I have learned what I don't want—and with Andre I have learned what I do want. When I was with the others, I saw them only as boyfriends. With Andre, I saw him first as a friend. When I was in the other relationships, I forgot everyone around me. Now that I am with Andre, I do not have to pretend to be someone I am not, and I can include my friends and my family responsibilities. In relationships, it's all about working together.

TEAM PLAYER
DANIEL MONROE

A team is a group of people that works together towards one ultimate goal. It may have a player who attracts all the attention, but in the long run, a team that actually works together without a star player will achieve more than anyone would have imagined possible. I believe that a team that relies on a star player will always depend on that player. He or she might lead the team to victories, but if the team lacks a solid foundation, all of those victories are worthless. This is true especially if the team members feel like they didn't have a hand in the team's success. As corny as it may sound, the statement that there is no "I" in "team" proves to be true.

A coach needs to know how to divide power evenly throughout the team while knowing each player's strengths and weaknesses. For example, from 1999 to 2004 Phil Jackson was the coach of the Los Angeles Lakers. The team won three championships, one right after another, but all of this soon changed.

During the Lakers' championship years, the two players who got the most praise were Shaquille O'Neal and Kobe Bryant. They learned to work together and accept the fact that each had his own place on the team. Their talents were implemented so that there was an equal balance of stardom. Kobe was good at three-pointers and crazy dunks, as well as having good crossovers; Shaq was mainly good at rebounding, jump hooks, and getting the ball in the hole. Together they were an unstoppable duo, and together they defined the Lakers as the best team in the NBA. Other teammates such as Derrick Fisher and Kareem Rush made the 2000–02 Lakers one of the best rosters in franchise history.

This year, the team's most essential players have left. Horace Grant, Brian Shaw, Robert Horry, and Derrick Fisher are all gone. Shaq has gone to Miami. Kobe is trying to be the "star," and Phil Jackson isn't the coach anymore. Some players have retired, but the fact is that the Lakers have split up. Each player played his part on the team, and that is what made them truly successful. Now they seem to have lost sight of that. What happened to the Lakers is a prime example of how a single person can never make up a team. Rather, a team is made up of people who are open-minded and devoted and who work hard.

There are a lot of differences between a star player and a team player; they are two completely different things. The difference is that a star player cares more about himself than he does his teammates. He feels he must take control whenever possible. A team player is the complete opposite because he is willing to sacrifice himself for his teammates. A star player wants to win but doesn't care about whether the team works together to do so. A team player feels like he makes up a fraction of the team and that only when everyone is in accord can the team really have any success.

Often teammates do not agree on some topics, and each feels that his ideas are best. I learned this firsthand earlier in the year. Our class had been assigned to split into groups and develop an idea for a start-up business. Everyone had different takes and opinions on the subject, and our assigned facilitator didn't feel much like leading. There were two researchers, one of whom, like Kobe and Shaq, was a star player; a facilitator like Rudy Tomjanovich, who was not doing much to improve the situation; and one recorder, Derrick Fisher, who represented me. One of the researchers and the facilitator wanted to go into the custom shoe industry. The other researcher didn't care what we did. I wanted to develop a custom car company. I was so frustrated because no one was listening. The so-called "leader" just wanted everything to be done his way. He paid no attention to the ideas of his teammates. That led to everything being a complete mess.

In our group, the leader and one of the researchers were like Shaq and Kobe. The other researcher was someone like (No Offense) Rick Fox—kind of lazy, passive, and unwilling to do his best for the team. This person did not express his opinion at all, and was there just for the hell of it.

This is representative of how the Lakers fell apart. They possessed two star players who had control over the team but occasionally misused their ability to take charge. On one hand, Shaq actually made the people around him, both teammates and opponents, play better, although he occasionally showed off. On the other hand, Kobe tried too hard to be the next Michael Jordan and wanted the team to be his, which ultimately ended up in Shaq leaving town.

In the end, we agreed to start a custom shoe business. Although our team wasn't exactly functional, this experience taught me how to be part of a team and convinced me to be more open toward others' ideas. It showed me what it felt like to be ignored and how every person's ideas should be taken into consideration.

More importantly, I learned that teammates should be so involved in their group effort that they no longer envision themselves as separate people but rather as one entity. This focus alone should eliminate the need for someone to become a star player. People need to be dedicated and have self-discipline. They need to be responsible for whatever role they play. Doing these things should help build the foundation for a team willing to make compromises, one that could agree to disagree. "A team with a star player is a good team. But a team without one is a great team." I couldn't have said it any better myself.

ÁNIMO BASKETBALL TEAM
TODD ANDERSON

Ánimo is a charter high school built to prepare students from diverse backgrounds for college through leadership, technology, and a rigorous curriculum. The teachers take time to make sure the students know the skills and strategies needed to understand ideas and to pass standardized tests. They make sure every student is actively involved in the lesson for the day. What Ánimo does in the classroom—will it work on the court?

It is Friday, January 14. The Ánimo JV and varsity basketball teams are sitting in a cramped and musty school bus climbing the hill on the way to games at Chadwick. On arrival, the JV basketball team hops off the bus and runs to the locker room to change. Once on the court, Coach Wilson says, "Let's go out there and win. It doesn't matter how." Coach Owens says nothing; he just sits down on the bench. Then Coach Wilson points to Rick, Sean, Joseph, Allen, and me, and tells us we are the starting five. The other three JV members sit on the bench. The whistle blows and echoes in the gym. It is time to start the game.

Rick jumps for us, and a big heavy kid wearing the number 32 jumps for Chadwick. The ball tips to Joseph, but instead of running a play, he jacks up a shot that bricks, and Chadwick runs it back for an easy layup. This continues for a few more minutes before Coach Wilson calls a time-out and puts Vince in for Joseph. With a new person on the floor, we hope to cut the lead. Our players pass the ball around a few times until we find Allen wide open for a three-pointer. He shoots: it's in. We have points on the board. For the rest of the half we struggle, going back and forth. It's not that the other team is better; it's that we can't make shots. We can't get into a set rhythm on offense. But this is a game we can win. All we have to do is play as a team.

The buzzer blares. It is halftime. In the locker room, Coach Owens starts by yelling the usual profanities at us. He hits the locker door and walks out of the locker room. While he shouts, I zone out. I don't want to hear about what went wrong, but rather what we can do to win the game. Then Coach Wilson says to us, "We've been in this situation before. We can come back and win the game. All you have to do is believe in yourself. What you can do is 95 percent mental and 5 percent physical. We can do this. All right, let's get back out there. HEART on three, HEART on me, 1 . . . 2 . . . 3 . . . HEART."

When Coach Wilson says, "Heart," it brings out a sense of pride. I can do this. I can make Ánimo proud. No, WE can do this. WE can work as a team. I hear the word echoing through the heart of Chadwick. We take the court in the third quarter, down by thirteen but energized by what the coach has said. It's Chadwick's ball: they take it out, but Allen steals the ball and runs down the court. He gives the ball to Joseph, who lays it up off the glass, slapping the backboard to show how high he can jump. We go on a big run in the third quarter because, for the first time in a long time, we are actually playing like a team. We make smooth passes; we set up plays and look for the open man.

Then Damon comes into the game. The Chadwick players see weakness and pass the ball to their center. The center does a head fake to get Damon in the air, then goes around him to score. Damon fouls him, so the center goes to the line and makes a three-point play. Sean starts yelling at Damon, "What is your problem? How did you let him score? You suck!"

RING!!! With the sound of the buzzer comes the end of the third quarter. Sean shouldn't have yelled at Damon the way he did. That wasn't right, especially for the team captain. Instead of tearing each other down, we should build each other up. This is teamwork at its worst.

For most of the quarter the teams battle for the lead, going back and forth like a pendulum. Then, in the final three minutes of the quarter, Coach Wilson calls a time-out. He subs Damon out. He puts me back in. I'm glad he thinks I can help the team win, but at the same time I'm also nervous that I might make a mistake that could cost us the game. Coach says, "We are in deep trouble. We're down by four and Chadwick has the ball. We need a stop on defense, then a score on offense. We are running man-to-man, so everybody knows who they have. When you are on the court, call out a number so everyone knows who they are guarding. Is that clear?"

We walk back on the court, calling out a flurry of numbers: "Thirty-four, fifteen, eight, three, nine." When Chadwick tries to pass the ball in, Joseph gets a steal and runs up court and CLACK, slaps the backboard. But the ball also hits the backboard—he has bricked the open layup. I grab the rebound and am instantly surrounded by Chadwick players. The coaches start yelling and call a time-out to yank Joseph. Joseph bows his head in shame. With Vince on the floor and Joseph on the bench, we get ready for the inbound. Sean gets the ball in successfully, then calls for it back again. He shoots a wide open shot. SWISH! Nothing but the bottom of the net. The gym goes quiet. Everybody has their eyes on the court.

With thirty seconds on the clock, Chadwick has the lead, 44 to 42, and the ball. They try to run down the clock. The point guard throws a bad pass, but it deflects off Sean's hand out of bounds. Coach Wilson calls a time-out and tells us, "OK, we need a steal to come out with the win, so everybody play man. Ánimo on me, Ánimo on three, 1 . . . 2 . . . 3 . . . Ánimo!" Chadwick tries to inbound the ball. The pass is intercepted by Allen, who calls the last time-out with only five seconds on the clock. The coaches tell us to do whatever it takes to win.

Sean passes the ball to Joseph. Joseph sees Allen up court, but instead of passing, he shoots a long three-pointer from half-court with a hand in his face. The buzzer sounds. A woman gasps for breath and the gym is quiet. The ball hits the back of the rim and drops to the floor. The gym goes crazy with sounds of excitement because Chadwick won the game.

This is a constant reality for the Ánimo JV basketball team. We can't win a game. The reason is a lack of teamwork during games and during practice. Our players don't get the ball to open people, or call out the plays when needed, or help out on the 2-3 defense. This lack of teamwork led to a season of one win and fourteen loses, which is horrible by anybody's standards. We want to win, but we can't seem to play together and function as a team.

LINKING MINDS AND LIVELY HANDS:
THE CREATION OF FILM
BRITTANEY BARBA

In the 1950 film *Sunset Boulevard,* screenwriter and director Billy Wilder states, through his character Joe Gillis, "Audiences don't know somebody sits down and writes a picture. They think the actors make it up as they go along." When people watch a movie, do they see the vision and effort of one mind or of many? Film requires a wide range of ideas, talent, and effort to create a final product that allows the creator's and audience's imaginations to run wild on screen.

Film has long been a passion of mine. The stories that come alive in front of my eyes enable me to escape reality and leap into my imagination. I appreciate the writer for creating the basic structure of a film, and I identify with the actor's character. Not only that, but every time a film ends I read the lengthy list of professionals, and I marvel at the number of people involved in putting it together. This has given me the idea of pursuing a career in the film industry.

Film is a collaborative art. The countless minds in front of the camera, behind the scenes, and inside the theater are the ones who invent and construct a movie. Every film begins with a story, which the scriptwriter transforms into a screenplay. Generally, a producer hires a writer to develop an idea, or a production company purchases the rights to a book, stage play, or account of a personal event. One example of this is the novelist Stephen King, whose books were made into horror classics like *The Shining* and *The Shawshank Redemption.*

The producer helps create the final film by working with the director and financing source to reach an estimated cost and budget. He or she also supervises the casting process and location scouting while assembling a shooting schedule. Irving Thalberg, an American producer, is most notable for his film *Grand Hotel,* starring Greta Garbo and John Barrymore, which won an Academy Award for Best Picture in 1932. He refused to credit himself on his films, with the exception of *The Good*

Earth. The production designer, art director, and set decorator also work with the director in designing the look of the film. Often, the art director is mistaken or identified as the production designer. The production designer works closely with the director and cinematographer, mobilizing the carpenters, painters, makeup and hair artists, wardrobe consultants, prop masters, and stunt men. The art director manages the time and money spent on construction, wardrobe design, special effects, and props. The set decorator is responsible for dressing up the set, translating the production designer's vision for each scene. A. Arnold Gillespie created the special effects used in *The Wizard of Oz*. The Kansas tornado was made by constructing a thirty-five-foot muslin stocking that was rotated by a speed-controlled motor. The cyclone's dirt and dust clouds contained dangerous chemicals like sulfur and carbon, and compressed air was used without proper ventilation.

The cinematographer focuses on the physical appearance of the film. Cinematographers are also known as "directors of photography." Their task is to coordinate the crew working with the lighting and cameras. They are responsible for the visible mood and tone of the film. They work with the director and actors during rehearsals to arrange the light level, color level, and focus. They also work with the camera operators, gaffers, and grips. The editor, meanwhile, works with the director after filming is completed to assemble scenes into a chain of events that flow. The editor can rearrange, remove, or re-create scenes. The editor also works with the music and sound effects editors.

The director oversees all the people and activities involved in making the final film. Above all, the director's task is to lead the actors and actresses on set. They have to figure out the way each scene will be shot and how the story will be told. Alfred Hitchcock and Steven Spielberg are among the greatest and most celebrated directors. Hitchcock is notorious for manipulating the leading ladies of his films like puppets, while Spielberg is beloved for his sci-fi and adventure masterpieces like *Jurassic Park* and the *Indiana Jones* series.

Filmmaking consists of a process of linking minds and lively hands. Without the unity and collaboration of these skilled professionals, the movies that we love could not exist. Audiences sit down in the dark as the screen's lights glow and become mesmerized by an unknown world.

HIS SPIRIT LIVES ON IN ME
GERALDIN PONCE

It is better to die on your feet than to live on your knees.
—The Legacy of a Revolutionary

The year is 1879. A boy is born in a small town in Morelos, Mexico. It's an average day like any other: the sun is out and the peasants work the haciendas. The townspeople go about their business but do not know that today one of the most important figures in Mexican history will be born. Emiliano Zapata, born to a middle-class family of mestizo heritage, will take his first breath in the cruel world.

Thirty years later, deprived of an education, he becomes the leader of his village and recruits fellow farmers into his army of radicals. Zapata's long struggle to overcome the hacienda owners and defend the rights of his people who are forced into peonage is just beginning. His passionate pleas for land and liberty are heard across Mexico. Zapata's sole purpose is to return the land to its rightful owners—the peasants of Mexico.

Years later, Porfirio Díaz, the dictator, is ousted from office, partially due to Zapata's forces and other insurgent armies. The tug-of-war for freedom is far from over. Francisco Madero takes over the presidential position, falls short of his promises, and is assassinated by a rival political party; a new leader seizes his position. Another long battle begins for Zapata and his followers, but they do not come out victorious.

On April 9, 1919, Zapata is ambushed and killed by General Guajardo for a bounty. General Guajardo, who cowardly lured Zapata into a trap, receives half of the bounty that had been offered. Zapata is gone, and though his ghost is said to have been seen riding with his army in the dead of night and during the bloodiest of battles, his army soon falls apart. Yes, Zapata is physically gone, but his radical ideals are far from diminished.

Although his crusades were not entirely successful, Zapata is still considered to be one of the most electrifying figures in Mexican history and an inspiration to many young revolutionaries today. Though it appears thar Zapata accomplished his fame and power on his own, teamwork actually played a large part. Many say that there is no "I" in "team," but the question arises: Why does one person often get more recognition than the whole? Just like Emiliano Zapata, many others died for the cause and struggled for liberation. The only difference is that Zapata organized them. While Zapata was, in fact, the leader, he never presented himself as superior to his followers. As evidence of this, he never took an official post in the government.

Many heroes are thought to be perfect beings without flaws, but the reality is that they are only human. Although Zapata was an amazing communicator and a great hero in Mexican history, he did have one flaw—the inability to negotiate and trust other groups. Zapata fought for the south, and another charismatic leader, Pancho Villa, fought for the north. Though they both battled towards a common cause, they never united. However, they did briefly come together during conferences. Zapata was stubborn, and though very passionate in the fight for land and liberty, he was not able to cede control. Many people betrayed him during his life, and this blinded him. His unwillingness to work together with different groups may have cost him the war. We can only speculate what might have happened if Zapata and Villa had joined forces, but it is logical to conclude that their chances of success would have increased if they worked as a team. Just as teamwork helped make Zapata what he was, his inability to work with other groups could have contributed to his failure.

Today, not much has changed in Mexico. A group of rebels in Chiapas formed to combat the same injustices Emiliano Zapata fought against. They are the Zapatista Army of National Liberation. They are the ones who carry on the legacy and spirit of Emiliano Zapata and his fellow soldiers. Although underestimated because of their indigenous backgrounds, they are a strong force in Mexican society and continue to grow and network. The fight for equality, land, and better living conditions is far from over, but as long as they continue to work as a team, a new revolution is not far away. Zapata has yet again united his people towards a common goal, and every day they grow stronger. The Zapatistas are not just a rebel group; they are the voices of the millions of indigenous people in Mexico.

Zapata and his Zapatistas have been more than just historical figures in my life. They lured me out of my secure box and introduced me to a world filled with social injustice. Though they did help me realize that the world is not always a perfect place, they also taught me that there is still hope and that the voice of the people is much stronger than the voice of individuals trying to bring them down. Their cause, their struggle, and their unity has helped define the person I want to become. I no longer want to be an individual standing on the sidelines but rather a part of a group fighting for what is right.

Zapata, and most importantly his cause, will never die until his people are granted the land and liberty that they rightfully deserve. He is a testament to what teamwork can accomplish on a grand scale. His spirit lives on in me and in every Zapatista and young revolutionary around the world. Whether we fight for small or massive causes, we always remember that, "It is better to die on your feet than to live on your knees!"

I am sitting here on this concrete floor, taking a glimpse of my life today. Birds sing, chirp. They live. I try to listen, but their sound dims as my mind drags me somewhere else. I don't want to go back, but the time dominates. The singing is transformed to a mutter of words. The brick walls, city trees, and concrete floor diminish against my will, converting to a lifeless scene. My eternal incarceration. The singing fades to murmurs, the vertical surfaces rise. My thoughts go from today to three years ago . . . My father's diagnosis. Kidney failure!

The blank hospital walls enclose me in a confinement that will forever haunt me in my dreams. I am imprisoned. A mirage appears, a door. Lines adorn the top of this door, symbolizing an exit. I run with anxiety to this door, to my escape. As I run to it, then through it, the realization hits me: it is just a door. It is no exit for me. There is no escaping it, so I do what I am forced to—face it! The steps to the door are dreadful and eternal. It is what seems to be a never-ending hallway. The symbol "357" is engraved with his blood and my tears. The antiseptic scent penetrates as I near. I am numb. My feet are moving, but I am not. I place my sight on a blurriness that is so clear.

Reality is like a burglar that doesn't affect you until you've been robbed. Walking into that room I became a victim of this burglary; I was left vulnerable.

"Mexicanos no se rajan!" This saying is famous in Mexican culture. It demands that no man ever show any weakness or any emotion—it is ingrained in Latino culture. Men will not show any type of emotion, whether it be good or bad. It is awkward for a Latino man to say "I love you" or to simply give a hug of affection. This doesn't mean that Mexican men are not loving; it is simply in their own nonphysical, nonverbal way. I have grown up in an environment where a pat on the back is the way of showing any emotion to a daughter by a father. There are the occasional

hugs due to a graduation or some type of congratulation. Those are rare! The words "I love you" are a foreign language to me! I grew up in a world where my father's presence was barely visible to my eyes or heart. He was either working all day or he would be dedicating time to "acquaintances" who, at the end, showed no loyalty. My everyday ritual: I would go to school, come home, be with my mom, and then go to sleep. My dad was nothing but the name on the bills and an empty space in my mom's bed. To me he was a stranger walking down the street who happened to know my name. This was my life for thirteen years. Then it changed . . .

There he was. The reality of it stung me like the venom of a snake. The image of this strong, independent man was shattered by the new reality of this weak, needy, male body. He was lying restless on this bed that confined him in so many ways. He was no longer able to live as free as he wished. His body was kept alive with these tubes that rotted the previous image of him. Those present were his family and—just his family. What happened to those "friends" my dad dedicated so much of "my" valuable time to? They showed their true identity: They weren't friends; they were just acquaintances that my dad spent all his time with instead of me. As I witnessed this scene, I drew near to get a better view. The sight was saddening yet mixed with a taste of sweet revenge. I felt sad about what was happening to my father, but I also had a smirk on my face about what was happening to this man.

Absence is conveyed as a feeling of hollowness. I experienced this absence for thirteen years of my life. There were times my dad was physically there, but no matter if he was there or not, this hollowness remained. When I lost my first tooth, the absence was there. When I got Student of the Month awards, the emptiness was present. When I experienced the transition from childhood to young adulthood, the ghost of him was not even visible. Through all those times I thank my mom and my sister for always being there through rain or shine. My mother and sister were there, but where was he? Although he was never there, I went on. There were times the pain weakened me, but thanks to those who truly loved me, it never defeated me. This was my childhood.

As I witness his agony, I realize I am somewhat satisfied with the justice that has been served. For you see, he was—and to this day is—getting a strong dose of the pain I endured for all those years (although, I will admit that a part of me feels sorry for the fact that it had to come down to this). Every day is a challenge for him, as well as for my mother, my sister, and me. Now the right person fills that empty space on my mom's bed, and that name on the bills now has a face. There was an absence of that whole family teamwork—and damn, it was needed. Those thirteen years would have been a hell of a lot easier if we were a true team. Now that he is closer to death, he is closer to us, his family! I have learned to forgive and forget. I will get no benefit from remembering. It is like they say, "Life is like a pen mark: you can scratch it out, but you can never erase it." We will never be able to recoup those thirteen years lost, but we're working on those that are left. It's hard to be a team, but the sacrifices are well worth it. We are now a true team. We now try to enjoy every minute possible with each other. I am just glad that my father realized in time that he has a family—before, well, it's too late.

I'm still sitting here on the concrete. The vibrant brick walls are declaring their stories. I have just declared mine. As I look back, I'm glad we're a family. It truly saddens me to think that my dad could die any day. It's been three years since his diagnosis. It's been thirty-six months of waiting on that list for a better life: a kidney transplant. I have learned the language of love; I understand what "I love you" means. However, this language has its limits for me. There are no constant hugs or constant reminders of love. We're Latinos, and as they say, *"Mexicanos no se rajan!"*

THE CHILD IN THE VILLAGE
MALLORY LESTER

It may take a village to raise a child, but I don't think that means just any village.

Being a child, you are curious to know what will happen if you call 911. Well, I called one night. My mom and dad were in the back room, and I was in the kitchen doing my homework right next to the phone. I dialed 911 and told them that I was home alone and then hung up the phone. Then 911 called and asked if there was a small child playing on the phone.

All hell broke loose.

My dad came into the room and yelled at my mom and me. He said that I knew what I was doing, was trying to get them in trouble. My father told my mom that she should spank me and send me to bed for a week without dinner.

The next day my dad came over and asked me if my mom had spanked me. He told me to tell the truth, because if I did not, he would spank me. So I told the truth, and said that my mom did not spank me. That's when they got into a big fight. If my mom never stands up for me ever again, I am glad that she stood up for me then. She told him, with head rolling and a finger waving, "You are not here all the time and when you are here, you act like you are running something up in here."

By this time I had already gone downstairs and was watching the TV. The fact that my mom and dad were fighting was nothing big, because they did it a lot. What my mom told him was true. He didn't live with us and only really came around when the T.O.M. (time of the month) was not visiting my mom.

As I was coming up the stairs, my dad was coming down. He looked at me and told me in his cold, deep voice, "Mallory, I am leaving, and it is entirely your fault." He looked down and saw that I had on the shoes he bought for me. Being the evil man that he was, he lifted up my leg, slid my shoe off, and took it and left. That was the last time that I saw my father. He left me there at the door looking stupid, with one shoe on and one shoe off.

He soon died of cancer.

I never felt any love for my father because I could hardly recall feeling any love from him. I always felt that he and I had to compete for my mom's attention.

All his ex-girlfriends and his current girlfriends came to his funeral with their kids, my half brothers and sisters; this was my first time meeting some of them. I had met one of his girlfriends before. She was light-skinned with short brown hair and hips that looked like they were going to bust out of her pants. She was totally different from my mom. My mom is kinda on the heavy side with honey-brown hair and not so tall. They were fake people telling lies about how good a man he was and how he changed their lives. Every once in a while my mom would burst out into a laugh and then have to act like she was crying.

Of all the lies they told, they never talked about the man that I knew. *I remember* the time that I was at that evil man's shop and he would make me stand in front of the African statues and the pictures that he knew scared me. *I remember* the evil man who beat me with horsetails and cords. *I remember* that evil man was my father.

It was so cold in the Angeles Funeral Home, yet I was so hot—hot because I was filled with anger and happy that he was gone, but I couldn't help feeling a little bit sad for the people who did love him and who he really loved. At the young age of seven, I knew what it felt like to hate. I only cried at his funeral because there were no flowers.

If I could say anything to my father, I would say that his stupidity and lack of parenting skills have changed the way that I feel about males. I can never really respect them because of the things that I had to go through as a child. It has affected my relationships with my male teachers and friends. I can't make eye contact with any men.

Although, it is getting better. My mommy does the best that she can with me. I want to tell her what I am going through and how I really feel about the past.

The village was there, the people were there, but they didn't really do their jobs. Any two people can have a child—but that does not make them real parents. Parents talk to each other; they don't let the other one put the child down. When push comes to shove, they at least act like they love each other. And they should always be there for you. Otherwise, what's the point of raising a child?

THE CLOCK WITH ONE HAND
RAQUEL BARRERA

When she was a baby, she learned to crawl on her own. She went from diapers to underwear faster, it seemed, than the speed of light.

"Cleo, you're much too young to start school. Slow down."

These were the words Cleo had heard as long as she could remember. Although she felt that preschool and kindergarten were unnecessary for her, she still had the urge to be a part of them. Her walls were covered with drawings, her shelves toppled over with books. Instead of learning the alphabet from a teacher, Cleo depended on her books, and only her books.

Cleo's parents loved her with a passion, but her need for solitude and her independent spirit left them in awe. Like many people, they feared what they didn't understand.

"I'm worried. It's not normal. She's so young."

As time passed and Cleo grew up, her parents became even more confused. Cleo was seventeen years old, and her parents' biggest fear was . . . . well, in their words:

"What if she has no friends? She's too young to be alone all the time!"

Little did they know that Cleo had befriended just about the whole school. When asked about Cleo, certain people's responses were:

"She's amazing. I wish I was like her."

"I adore her. She's unique." And . . .

"I would go out with her, but she deserves better."

She seemed perfect. Yes, that's the word . . . perfect. But not to all. When asked about Cleo, other people's responses were:

"I don't like her. She's not normal."

"What's with her? No one's that perfect." And . . .

"I would never go out with her; she thinks too much of herself."

By age seventeen, Cleo had many admirers. She had had boyfriends, but none were ever serious. To her, a boyfriend was simply a symbol representing who she was: a normal teenager.

One night Cleo lay in bed, her friend Maggie's words playing over and over in her head.

"What are you scared of? You like him . . . take a chance."

"No, it's just a silly crush," she had responded.

"I have never seen you act this way about a 'silly crush.' Cleo, please. Take a chance with him."

In the dark silence she whispered to herself . . .

"Why not?"

His name was Damien Thatcher. He was eighteen and planned to take a year or two off before attending a prestigious university, with the hope of seeing the world with a fresh pair of eyes.

As Mr. Hall discussed World War II, Damien and his friend Jake had something else on their minds.

"She likes you, and you like her."

"Oh right. She likes ME?"

"I've known Cleo since she was walking circles around me in preschool. I have never seen her give those eyes to another guy. I say go for it."

Damien stared at Cleo across the room, in the only class he was lucky enough to share with her. He knew what had to be done when she shot him back a glance that left no need for words.

After school, Cleo decided she had waited long enough and had to take matters into her own hands. When she spotted Damien walking home, she ran up to him and said gently, as though she hadn't just run six blocks for him:

"Do you want to go out with me?"

Before they knew it, the flowers bloomed, their eyes sparkled, and the clouds parted. Damien Thatcher was now officially going out with Cleo Burciaga.

They were soon inseparable. Cleo's parents had to face the music that their only child was no longer lonely. This alarmed her parents more than before, when she was on her own.

"I'm worried. It's not normal to be with someone so much. She's too young."

They feared low grades, rebel behavior, and surprise pregnancies. Although they were very unhappy with her new boyfriend, they decided to let things be because they knew that Cleo was a smart girl who would never jeopardize her future for some boy.

It soon became apparent, though, that Damien was not just "some boy" to Cleo. Her phone consistently rang at sunrise and she awoke to the sound of his voice. She often left a mix CD for him that expressed her feelings for him at the time. He left letters in her locker if he hadn't talked to her for more than an hour. These small gestures revealed just a glimpse of their passion for one another.

Six months passed, and to Cleo's shock, the butterflies lasted. Feelings of boredom with one another or being trapped never surfaced.

Still, six months later, when the phone rang Damien and Cleo each had a minor heart attack in hopes that it was the other calling. The strange thing was, Damien seemed to accept the fact that Cleo had to have things her way. He realized that she had always been that way and that there was no point in trying to change her.

Cleo, on the other hand, soon realized that she was not the only one who thrived on independence. After spending so much time together, Cleo saw that Damien also wanted to have things his way—though he'd never say so.

This became apparent when she was assigned to work on a history project with him. Cleo had spent the whole night working on the project. The next day, when Damien came over after school and found the project completely finished, Cleo saw pure disappointment on his face.

"I stayed up all night, but it was worth it."

"Cleo . . . you didn't have to do this, you know."

"I wanted to. I had a million ideas running through my head and figured I might as well."

Damien walked away and softly whispered to himself, "I had a few ideas, too."

Cleo was bothered and stunned by his reaction. She had spent so much time on the project, yet he seemed irritated by the fact that she had given him an easy A. There had never been a time when one of her partners objected to her doing all the work. Damien never said a word about it, and Cleo filed the memory away.

After a year, the butterflies remained, and even though Damien and Cleo knew they were madly in love, those words had never rolled off their tongues.

When December brought heavy rain, everything changed. It was the Winter Formal, and the smell of clean air filled everyone's lungs. With Cleo in an elegant dress and Damien in a sharp suit, the night promised to be great. When the band began to play their song—a cheesy love song—Cleo decided they would celebrate their one-year anniversary with a slow dance. Then Cleo made the mistake of taking the lead.

"What are you doing?" he asked.

"What do you mean?"

"Everything was going just fine. Why do you always have to lead?"

"Excuse me. I . . . I just . . ."

"No! That's it. I can't do this anymore. This relationship is all about you. If you'd ever let me have a say, you might find that I'm capable of many things."

Suddenly, all eyes were on Cleo. The few people at school who hated her for being perfect smirked at the fact that it was this very perfection that was destroying her relationship.

Damien stormed out of the dance hall, and Cleo stood there feeling as though someone had slapped her. Was it really over?

For weeks Cleo and Damien did not exchange a word. Each morning, Cleo's phone was silent. She no longer had someone waiting for her after class, and it scared her. In history class, every time she shot a glance at Damien, tears filled her eyes. Unable to stand it anymore, Cleo ran out of class. Damien knew what he had to do, because it was what he wanted to do: he ran after her.

In a deserted girl's bathroom, Cleo and Damien faced each other. Tears ran down Cleo's cheeks and Damien stood there, stunned. Not once in all their time together had Damien ever seen Cleo sad, let alone crying.

"I'm sorry. Cleo, you have to understand where I'm coming from. I feel like you never need me, but I still shouldn't have yelled at you."

Damien had to tell her everything he was feeling. He knew he had to get her back.

"I love you."

"No. I don't need to hear that now. Don't be sorry, it's all for the best. I . . . I can't be with you."

"What? Why?"

"Damien, ever since I was little I've done just about everything on my own. When we were together . . . well . . . when it came to an end, I realized that a relationship is not what I need right now. I'm sorry."

Cleo left before Damien had time to respond. It was just as well, since she had managed to leave him speechless.

Miraculously, the sun was out, but it didn't match anyone's mood. Cleo lay in bed, and for the first time in her life, she hated herself. Cleo's parents wandered the halls; hearing her sobs, they couldn't help but say:

"I'm worried. It's not normal to be so sad. She's too young."

The realization that Damien was good to Cleo and good for Cleo hit her parents. They knew the only way to mend her broken heart was to get him back. But that seemed impossible.

Cleo had lied to Damien and ruined everything. What she really wanted to tell him was that she realized how much she loved him and that it scared her. Cleo saw how dependent she had become on him. It was a strange feeling that she despised, adored, and somehow needed. That night she hardly slept, but she decided that she had to do something as soon as possible.

The next week, as Cleo walked home, she noticed how blue the sky was, how fluffy the clouds were, and how gently the wind was blowing. Just as her thoughts were drifting away, a bright yellow paper posted on a pole caught her eye:

The Clock with One Hand

She has the hand that guides us. In each and every way.
Without her we would never know the hours of the day.
Independent and alone she marks light our way.
I wish I could be the minutes to the hours of her day.
But until that day comes I'll love the hand on my lonely clock.
And if I'm ever lucky I will be the tick to her tock.

Cleo immediately knew that it was Damien who had written the poem about her. She looked around and the paper with the amazing poem was tacked to every single pole, up and down the street.

Cleo realized that she didn't have to do everything alone, and if their relationship was going to work she had to realize that it's give and take. For the first time in her life she was a part of a team—a team that, years later, even when times got tough, would always stay together.

My name is Elise Thatcher, and I am the daughter of Cleo and Damien Thatcher who are now resting in peace at the Saint Ives Cemetery. They spent the rest of their lives together. I was fortunate enough to find my mother's diary that tells the story. I've shared it with you because it's the story that helped me understand that love requires teamwork. I am married now, and though the independent spirit I inherited from my mother takes over at times, I am open to every possibility. Especially love.

THE SPECTER
MINDY GARLAND

I feel like an apparition gazing upon the place.
The fire rips and tears the building right down to the base.
The faces of desperate people finding out they don't have wings.
The water and the hoses become such small and useless things.

With wordless pleas I pray to build the water's flow and power.
My hands and mouth are useless as I watch closely every hour.
But I see myself in all of this, being a part of this whole team.
The survival of the masses is in the core of this team's dream.

The red-and-yellow licensed men have come to save the town.
But the wish of the fire going down appeared not to be found.
I became so faithless and my eyes go down, but I still can't walk away.
Looking at these fighters, my heart goes higher; I feel a blessing
coming on today.

The men were caked in ashes, but their hope was shining bright.
Even though they seemed so small from the burning fire's light.
They worked with such a diligence although the time was
running down.
And then below the distant blueless sky, the fire trucks come around.

The strength in numbers was profound, it evened out the odds.
A miracle was taking place, as if they were helped by the gods.
These savers of lives and knights of tales told rely on each other.
And it all pays off with smiles and cheers when a child is returned
to its mother.

The devil's fire is transformed now into a single spark.
And the sky returns to a bright blue hue, turning away from
that defeating dark.

With pep in my flow, I'm starting to glow at this happiness I feel.
Who knew in this cold and dreadful world true miracles were real.

On September 11, 2001, a tragic event transpired in the United States. Terrorists took over passenger-filled planes and crashed into the Twin Towers in New York City and the Pentagon in Washington, D.C. Approximately 3,000 people died by fire, suffocation, jumping out of the buildings, or from structures collapsing on their backs. I recently saw a photo of firemen in action during September 11th. They worked so hard to try to save those in danger, and you could feel and see the determination in the photo.

In this poem I tried to capture what I saw and felt in that single photo. It amazed me how much determination and love for the victims those firefighters must have had. Those heroes challenged death because they were unafraid, and they tried to save those in danger so they could be reunited with their families.

I dedicate this piece to all the heroes in our great nation.

As the golden bus pulled up to Warren Lane Elementary, the good-byes of the day's departure filled the air. I crossed the street with my best friend Aysia to my granny's house. Although the porch light was still on and the mail towered out of the mailbox, it never occurred to me that something wasn't right. Aysia and I decided to go around the corner to her house. Her mother's soulful cooking always welcomed guests. When we walked through the door, the familiar scents of African spices ignited the thought that something was wrong. I asked for the phone and the numbers flowed from my fingers like they always did. 757–8830. Five rings, then the answering machine, and I lost it.

"Where is she?" The sound of my voice surprised me as I spoke aloud without noticing.

"Her car was gone. Maybe she went to the store." Aysia tried her best to calm me, and the African spices worked their black magic again.

The numbers streamed out once more. This time my uncle picked up, and I was instantly pacified. "You better come home," he said. The walk back was familiar, but as I turned the corner, I didn't realize that I was leaving my childhood behind.

Suddenly, twelve years old seemed so much older. I was slightly myopic to my evolution from adolescence to a more mature individual, and I wouldn't recognize that for another four years.

The bright red-and-white ambulance burns hot in my memory . . .

It sat parked in a spot where it had never been before. Usually it was two houses down for the man with Alzheimer's, or across the street at the school. But this time it kissed the curb outside my granny's mint-green duplex. In an instant, 8th Avenue became my racetrack, and no one could stop me. Not Aysia or the paramedics. Not even the guy in the maroon van who almost hit me when I sprinted across the street. It was unreal. I was unreal—and before I knew it, I was on my knees on our lawn.

I watched, hysterically, as they wheeled my granny to the ambulance on a stretcher. My helplessness got the best of me, and my tears became too vivid to ignore. Still unable to fathom the situation, I remembered that my uncle was home, and he appeared as if I had imagined him to be there. His emotionless expression didn't match the potent hug that seemed to last for years. Never had a hug contained so much meaning.

We walked inside the house, and the smell of coffee suffocated me. It drowned the air and appeared to cover the walls. Dried coffee stains led from the kitchen to the bathroom and trailed off into the bedroom, where my uncle had found my grandmother. She had suffered a stroke and fell to the floor, spilling her morning coffee, then overturning her coffeemaker. She managed to get up and lumber from room to room until she finally reached her bed. There she lay, with the covers up to her neck. When my uncle came home, that's how he found her, her eyes rolled back in her head because she was having a seizure.

Because it was late in the afternoon when he found her and by the way the coffee stains had dried, we guessed she had been unconscious for five or six hours. Her brain grew more and more damaged as time progressed. If my uncle hadn't come home that day, my granny would not have made it.

My grandmother and I were very close, but after the stroke we all suffered. Of course, she suffered the most. Her vision was impaired, as well as her speech and mobility. Our family's relationships were put to the test as life's rotation shifted. Still, our love could not be stronger. The bond between my granny and me is the one thing that was affected positively by this tragedy.

My granny is my best friend. There's nothing in the world that could stop me from helping her, except for my age. It's the same for my sister and my younger cousin, Destiny. They were both six when it happened, and youth disables us from doing a lot of things. So we give her our love.

We spent countless days by her side and made numerous visits to the convalescent homes that she often found herself in. Spending the weekend at her house became so typical that my friends began to call me there. We constantly encouraged her to think about what she was trying to say, as if we were her personal speech therapists, her motivation and reasons for living.

"Slow down. Granny, it'll come to you," I would say.

Her response was always the same: "I know, but it's so hard."

My sister, my cousin, and I have become closer because of these frequent interactions. Cooking and cleaning became habits almost as natural as breathing. Private jokes about Granny's speech—a guilty pleasure— kept us laughing all night long. Most of the time Granny laughed right along with us.

Her laugh never changed; neither did her bad habits. She can't always get our names right, but she'll never forget how to ask for a cigarette.

Slowly but surely, her speech began to recover, and it became a lot easier to understand her. It took some time, but she speaks a lot better now than she did in 2001 when it happened.

To me, teamwork is a vital aspect of life that is needed for survival. Lack of teamwork can become so dangerous and deadly that it's impossible to survive. I think the love and determination behind Destiny, my sister, and myself is what allows my granny to live every day. It has been almost four years since the day of her stroke, and she is still alive. Her speech has become a lot better, and our conversations are endless.

THE INHUMANITY IN THE GANGS
ROCIO GAMEZ

One day in the summer, in broad daylight, my brother, his friend Luis, and I were walking just a few blocks from school. It was chilly, about three o'clock in the afternoon. We were waiting for our ride, my mom's friend who always picked us up after school. It was just like any other day in Inglewood. I was thinking about a school assignment. The boys were making jokes with each other. This was our routine. Luis and my brother said, "Later," and Luis crossed the street to get to his house.

Then, before we knew it, a couple of Hispanic guys wearing baggy clothes walked up to Luis. One guy with bad acne, about fifteen, looked like a wannabe gangster in faded jeans and a white T-shirt. The other, a couple of years older, looked like a real gang member in all black with baggy jeans and a hoodie, which made him look tough. Luis started to back away, trying to get to his house. I started to get worried; I knew something bad was going to happen. The real-looking gang member reached for Luis's back pocket to see if he had money or a cell phone, because that's what most gang members are after. Luis just stood there, not refusing. I saw the guys counting some money as they walked our way.

They asked my brother, "Where you from," meaning what gang is he in. My brother didn't respond. He didn't seem worried and wasn't even mad. This happens to him a lot because gangs surround our neighborhood near Centinela Park. One of the guys checked my brother's pockets and they grabbed his wallet and took the twenty dollars that my dad had given him. They left by saying what gang they were from, claiming their neighborhood and thinking that this was their territory.

I felt angry, but I couldn't do anything. I also felt sad because I started to think to myself, what's the point of causing harm to others? You never know if guys like that might have a gun. If my brother would have refused or gotten in a fight with the guys, maybe the next day they would've brought more of their gang members and searched for us to do something even worse.

Experiences like this make me wonder why gangs exist. In L.A., there are approximately 416 gangs with some 46,187 members. Why do people join these gangs? They join because it's like another family to them, one that defends them. They join because they feel lonely and because they want to feel a part of something. They want to look tough in front of their friends. The community plays a role in why people join gangs, because some feel rejected from that same community.

Do all the gang members cause problems and do harm to others? According to a staff writer from the Los Angeles *Daily News*, "an estimated 4 to 10 percent of gang members are responsible for most of the city's violence."

I'm part of a gang—they defend me, keep me company, and make me feel a part of something. It's my family, my brother, my mom, and my dad. In my family, we have fun together. We laugh and even make jokes with each other. Most importantly, we communicate with each other. Almost every Saturday, my family and I go out to places to spend time with each other. We just talk and enjoy the day by having fun. My relationship with my parents leads me to believe that the main reason why people join gangs is because of their parents. They don't get the attention or love they want from their parents. Maybe their parents just work all the time and don't have the time to be there for them. They don't communicate with their parents and start to feel resentment toward them. Maybe this is why they join gangs and cause problems. They want to try to take their pain away by harming others.

Why can't gangs do good things for the community? Each gang-related murder costs taxpayers about $1.75 million; in five years the total is about $5.2 billion. If gang members would do good things for the community by helping, instead of vandalizing people and things, our community would be a much safer place. Instead of causing problems, they could get involved in sports, clubs, and other types of positive activities. I think people would feel safe if gangs stopped their violence and worked together to help others. If this happened, the community would be a better, more peaceful place.

MY FAMILY, MY SCHOOL, MY HOME
ZOROBABEL PRUNEDA

It was the summer after my freshman year in high school when I started to see my classmates as brothers and sisters. My teachers were still my teachers, but they were also now my friends. Everyone at my school was close, but it wasn't until that hot July day that we realized how deep our bond was. I think I speak for my classmates when I say that it was that summer that made my high school class become a true family. It wasn't school anymore—it was home.

Before I tell you about how my school became a family, I have to let you know that my high school is a charter school. This means that we are not like most other high schools. Charter schools are great because their main focus is the student's education. They have small-sized classes in order for the teachers to have more interaction with each student, and their main goal is to get students to college.

In my school there are 140 students for each grade level. So far we only have three classes: freshmen, sophomores, and the very best, juniors. I, with the rest of my classmates, will be the first graduating class of this high school. We are the founders of Ánimo. We were the ones who started this journey, and we will be the first to leave it in order to begin a new one. Everyone who has been here since the start knows how hard we have worked, and still work, to be what we are: the best!

When we first got to Ánimo we were greeted by our principal, Ms. dJ. She and the rest of the staff were determined to make this school a great success. She talked about the expectations she had for our school. She made it clear from the beginning that our school would become our family. I don't think anyone believed her at that moment; it just sounded corny. Half the students who came to Ánimo were there because their parents made them come. Others thought that this would be a better high school than the rest, and some students just came because they heard that our school was going to provide laptop computers. No one really thought that Ms. dJ's words would come true. Many of us had come from failing middle schools, schools that took no interest in us at any level. We didn't expect any more from this school. We thought they were just sweet talking us and that in a couple of weeks the school would come crashing down. We were wrong.

It seemed like the most boring school to be at those first few months, but it wasn't. We were spoiled. We had a gorgeous patio, one of the best places to hang out. We also had a game room; it had a ping-pong table, a radio, card games, and comfy couches. Lunch was fun and the food was great. Our teachers were also great. They were very patient, and up to this day they don't give up on us. They care so much about us on an academic level and a personal level. They have truly become our second parents. It wasn't hard for us to become close as the year passed us by. After all, there were a small number of students and teachers, so you couldn't help but get to know each other.

That year I got to know all of my classmates, and they also got to know me. Our population was half Hispanic, half African American, and one Caucasian. There were never any race problems at our school; we all got along fine, maybe because our school emphasized how important it was to look beyond our color. Or maybe because we became friends, so the color of our skin was never important—it just became invisible. We forgot about our race and we learned about what was inside us, our personality and our passions.

Our high school class has so many memories from that year. All the "small incidents" in the mornings in the patio, the fights, and the crazy things that our teachers would do to get our attention in class, like the time our principal, our English teacher, and our history teacher stood in front of the classroom to read and act out a poem. Our class couldn't stop laughing as they made hand movements and recited the chorus at the same time. They looked so funny up there that they grabbed our attention. I think the class will never forget about the Gold Rush, tectonic plates, or the way Boo Radley looked in *To Kill a Mockingbird*. It was a great year and to many it has become unforgettable.

Towards the end of the first year, most of us had become friends. We had good relationships, and we knew a lot about each other. The last day of school everyone signed yearbooks and said their good-byes. We knew we would see each other after summer vacation. Some would actually see each other during summer school. Right after we were dismissed, we took off.

A week passed by, and then summer school started for some students. The summer heat was intense that year, but it didn't hold anyone back from having fun. But the worst happened one day during summer school. One of our classmates shut his eyes forever. Sergio, who had let me borrow his ID holder so I wouldn't get detention that rainy day, and who I talked to many Wednesday mornings while he listened to Bone Thugs-N-Harmony, didn't come back for our sophomore year.

Sergio was one of the three people at my high school, including me, who had attended the same middle school. The first time I talked to him I asked him why he had come to Ánimo instead of going to the high school most of the students from our middle school attended. He told me that he had just ended up at Ánimo.

No one at our school is popular; we are so small that we all know each other, yet some people are more social or well known than others. Sergio was the quiet type; he had his friends, but he didn't talk to everyone. I had Sergio in three of my classes. In English he sat in the yellow desk up at the front, but he was shy and didn't speak much. In Technology he sat by the window in one corner, very silent. Oh, but in Spanish, Sergio was someone different. He and some of the other guys would constantly get in trouble for misbehaving. I remember he would throw spitballs at me and some of the girls just to make us mad; it worked sometimes. Unfortunately, Sergio was moved out of my Spanish and English classes so I would only see him in the mornings on the patio and in technology class. The spitballs were gone.

He was one of my friends, but I remember that towards the end of the year he and I didn't talk as much. The only times we would hang out was in the mornings, with the rest of the guys, and Wednesdays since we would come to school early. The last time I saw him was at my sister's middle-school graduation, a couple weeks before he passed away.

Summer school had already started and Sergio was one of the students who had to go. As Sergio walked home one day after summer school, he was shot by a gang member not too far away from where I live. It was said that his heart stopped beating on his way to the hospital.

I found out about Sergio's death the day after he was shot. The students at summer school were the first ones to know, and the rest of the students and parents found out by a letter sent by Ms. dJ. The day I found out I woke up late; it was summer and the sun was out early. I wasn't supposed to go to summer school, but Ms. dJ had called me a few days earlier to ask if I would give a speech at the inauguration of another Ánimo school. I carried a blue journal that my friend and I had started that summer, and I was wearing my uniform. When I got to school, a new security guard met me as I was on my way up the stairs. He asked me why I was at school, and I told him about my speech. He told me to go right ahead, but before that he mentioned that a lot of things were going on at school and that I had to be quiet. As I went up the stairs to go into Mr. Sotelo's classroom, I found my mentor, Ms. Simmons. She said hi, and I asked her what was going on.

"One of your classmates, Sergio—you know him?"

"Yeah," I replied, a little impatient.

"Well, he was shot yesterday."

I can't remember what I felt at that point, but it was as if she had said nothing to me. I must have looked like a fool, but I didn't understand her words.

"But he's fine. He's in the hospital, right?"

At that moment the thought of death didn't cross my mind, and this probably made it harder for Ms. Simmons to tell me.

Right after I asked her that, my friend Pablo—a real good friend of Sergio—came out of a room. He sat on the stairs with no emotion, just looking at the air. I turned to Ms. Simmons and she said it.

"I'm sorry, Zoro, he didn't make it. He passed away yesterday."

She began to rub my back since she could say no more, and then it came, the tears. She asked me if I would be OK and I said yes, so she went her way and I went into the room. I left Pablo on the stairs. I knew he wanted to be alone. When I walked in I just took a seat at an empty desk. There were tissues all over the place, and my friends were brainstorming ideas to help Sergio's family with the funeral; instead of having class that day, they were finding ways to help Sergio's parents. After the class was over, I, with some other students, took the bus to the inauguration of the new school. I gave my speech, came home, and cried in the bathroom.

I started going to summer school every other day to help out. We were notified when the viewing and Sergio's funeral would be. I went to both, like many of my classmates did. The viewing was very emotional. Everyone was wearing black, or like me, a T-shirt with Sergio's picture on it. My friend Anel and I walked into the room and recognized many familiar faces. When we went up to see Sergio's body, I was surprised, and in a way, relieved: the sad boy was not Sergio; at least, it didn't look like him. I wanted to turn around and tell everyone that it wasn't Sergio, that we had all been mistaken, that Sergio was not dead. Yet the tears in their eyes said otherwise. I got close to my friend. We all stood next to each other. We cried together and we leaned on each other for support.

When Sergio's funeral came, most of the students were there. We were still on vacation, yet so many of them showed up that one bus wasn't enough. Some of the teachers and some of the parents had to drive their cars. It was surprising: Sergio was not a very social person at school, yet so many of his peers showed up to say good-bye. It was amazing. We first attended mass. Everyone took a seat, and the priest started right away. He was also surprised to see so many students. I was also surprised when later I found out that when we took a seat at mass, Latinos didn't just sit with Latinos and that African Americans didn't just sit with African Americans—the majority of the time at school this would be our separation. It wasn't because of our race that we didn't hang out together; it just so happened that the people we were closer to were the same color. When I found out that this had occurred at church, I felt that we had really come together as a family. Ms. dJ's words weren't corny anymore. They were real.

After mass we went to Sergio's burial. It was the saddest feeling I've ever felt, yet it was so comforting to know that I had many of my friends to lean on. Many of us cried until our eyes couldn't take it anymore. I couldn't help but think that Sergio didn't want to leave. At his burial, white balloons were let go as a symbol of his spirit going up to heaven, yet the balloons ran into a tree nearby and got stuck. Then Sergio's dad released a dove, but the little creature wouldn't fly away; it seemed scared, as if it had not yet learned how to fly. I couldn't help the tears. I felt as if it were Sergio's way of saying that he didn't want to go, how he wasn't ready and how he longed to stay. I recall that someone said it was time for us to say our last good-byes. I held a tissue that someone had given me earlier, and then I walked away from the crowd. We had to go, so I started walking to the bus. On the way, I saw one of my friends sitting there with his face buried inside his shirt crying nonstop, I sat with him and rubbed his back; his face was still covered as if he felt shame about his tears. He was a boy, and "boys don't cry." But just like many others, he couldn't help it.

Unfortunately, no one could go back in time, and Sergio was laid to rest. His spirit never left Ánimo, and I know he is constantly in our thoughts. After his death many things changed. Not only did we realize that we are a family, we also say it like Ms. dJ said the first day of school. Everybody seemed to show love for each other even more, and everyone seems to have more pride as the Class of '06. Little things have changed, too: many of the people associated with gangs started to think more about the consequences. Our school became more rigid on anything that related to gangs—it was no longer tolerated. We didn't want anyone or anything to hurt our family again.

If you haven't figured it out, this event is one of the many reasons why my school became a family. It wasn't the best way, but it happened. Now we work together as a team. We back each other up and have learned to love one another. I have personally learned many things about my brothers and sisters. I not only know their favorite rappers and colors, I also know what makes them unique and beautiful. I love my school so much that when I think of graduating, I just want to hold back time. I have learned so much about everything and everyone at my school that I will not be able to forget any moment.

They say your college years are the best years of your life, but I just can't help doubting it. I still have senior year to go, and I know that after I graduate my school will keep growing stronger. I think I will look back on my experiences at Ánimo and realize that they were the best years of my life. After all, my class has left the best legacy at this school. We have built a family, and we have made a new definition for it. At my school family isn't about the people who share your blood, it's about the ones who share your passions, your biggest moments, your success, and your failures, the ones who lean on you for support and the ones you lean on when you need help. They're your best friends, the people you don't just hear but the people you listen to. They're the people who become a part of you and mean the world to you. This is my family, my school, my home.

SOME WHO HELPED WITH THIS BOOK:

These adults helped shape and edit the works contained within this book.

Adam Baer writes frequently for the *Los Angeles Times, Travel and Leisure,* and other publications.

Anne Fishbein is a fine-art and commercial photographer. Her work can be found in the collections of The Museum of Modern Art, the National Gallery of Canada, Musée Niépce, and the Los Angeles County Museum of Art. Perceval Press published her monograph *On the Way Home.* She is represented by Farmani Gallery in Los Angeles and Printworks in Chicago.

Lynell George is a features writer for the *Los Angeles Times* and is author of the book *No Crystal Stair: African Americans in the City of Angels* (Verso/Anchor).

Annette Gonzalez is in her eighth year of teaching at the middle- and high-school level. Prior to teaching at Ánimo, she taught in the Santa Monica–Malibu Unified School District and is a nationally board-certified teacher. She is a graduate of University of California Riverside and was a member of their NCAA softball team. She currently coaches Ánimo's varsity softball team. She has a passion for introducing her students to literature and the joys of reading a good book.

Cara Haycak has an MFA in creative writing from Columbia University; her first novel, *Red Palms,* was written for teens and was published by Random House in 2004. She is currently at work on her second book.

Tami Mnoian is a writer and editor who has recently tried her hand at teaching and directing music videos.

Allen Monroe II is a child of our nation's capital, but he has called

Inglewood, California, home for most of his life. Allen has been teaching English and coaching basketball in his community for the past three years and loves what he does. He believes that Team Jackson has been an excellent opportunity for his students to thoroughly analyze the impact that working together has on our society and to come to the realization that ethnicity doesn't matter because we need each other as Homo sapiens if man as a species is going to progress and survive.

Pilar Perez is Executive Director of 826LA. She has made many books in her career and is very proud to be publishing *Rhythm of the Chain.*

Sherri Schottlaender is a freelance editor who lives in San Diego with her husband Brian and Tallulah Mae, the Wonder Dog. When she's not obsessing about commas and subject/verb agreement, she can usually be found tending her garden or reading a good book.

Jervey Tervalon is the author of *Understand This* and the winner of the New Voices Award from Quality Paper Book club. He teaches at the Bunche Center for African American Studies at UCLA.

David L. Ulin is the author of *The Myth of Solid Ground: Earthquakes, Prediction, and the Fault Line Between Reason and Faith,* and the editor of *Writing Los Angeles: A Literary Anthology.*

Deborah Vankin is a writer/editor at the *L.A. Weekly* and she has authored chapters in the books *Based on a True Story . . . But With More Car Crashes* (a collection of essays on film), and the forthcoming *Taschen's Los Angeles.*

Melinda Viren is a native Californian and the tenth-grade English teacher at Ánimo Inglewood Charter High School. She has written for *PC World, Trans World Skate, E!Online,* and *Internet Underground.* She prefers molding young minds to interviewing celebrities about their websites. When she was twelve she was accused of swallowing a thesaurus; she took it as a compliment.

ABOUT THE AUTHORS:

 ARIANA ACEVEDO was born in Culver City, California. She loves to dance and be herself.

ARACELI ALVAREZ is seventeen years old and is a unique individual who sees life from a different perspective: through a 50mm lens. Music and photography are what surround her and make her who she is today. She dreams of taking her talents to the next level.

 JENNIFER ANDERSON is a junior at Ánimo Inglewood Charter High School. She aspires to become successful in all her endeavors. Hard working and motivated, she will one day positively contribute to her family and community.

 TODD ANDERSON is a hard working, African-American male trying to make it to UCLA. He enjoys playing basketball.

 FARRIN BAILEY is a young aspiring poet. She is original, outspoken, unique, beautiful, and will never be duplicated.

CINDY BALLÓN, seventeen years of existence, social, blah blah blah. Her guideline: "I don't know the key to success, but the key to failure is trying to please everybody" (Bill Cosby).

BRITTANEY BARBA was born in Santa Monica and raised in Inglewood, California, for most of her fifteen years of life. She is a Mexican-Danish American and a Sagittarius. Her interests include art, literature, music, and film; she is not obsessed with anything or anyone, unlike many of the teenagers her age.

 RAQUEL BARRERA is a person with many great passions in her life: music, film, family, and friends. She says, "I'm a dreamer, and though reality is not at times all I want it to be, it's all worthwhile when I hear an amazing song, watch an amazing movie, or spend time with an amazing person."

 VALERIE CORRAL is an independent and intelligent young lady anxiously waiting to put her mark on society. Her story is dedicated to those who feel they have to be someone they are not.

JESSICA CRUZ was born on July 10, 1990, in Lynwood, California, but raised in Inglewood. "I love to hang out with my friends and hear music from Green Day. I would like to attend USC, and I thank my mom Clara for always being there for me."

 DANIELA DOWELLS is a sixteen year old who loves her mommy and baby sis, Shorty, and Bugs Bunny.

GABRIEL GAMEZ, seventeen, is a Mexican American who writes poems for leisure. He uses life and the everyday struggle of living in the 'hood, "Inglewood," as his inspiration. Apart from this project he plays football and is a member of MEChA.

 ROCIO GAMEZ is a fourteen-year-old girl who lives in Inglewood and is nice and proud of being a Chicana. She is always happy and enjoys being with her friends. Her favorite color is blue, and she loves to shop.

GABINO GARCIA believes that too much censorship is a crime in itself. The overall message is sometimes lost, which is a crying shame.

MINDY GARLAND is driven, fierce, and determined: a true definition of an Aries. Often happy and always on her path, she proves that a lifelong cynical person can be born again optimistic.

 SANDRA GONZALEZ likes playing volleyball, tennis, and swimming. She dreams of becoming a lawyer. Nothing is ever too much for her to overcome.

 ASHLEY GRUBBS is seventeen years old and was born in Los Angeles, California. She enjoys playing basketball, writing, and reading, and looks forward to becoming a famous writer.

 ALLISON HOWARD was born in Inglewood, California. She believes that with God on her side, all things are possible. She motivates herself with her dream of being the female Ice Cube, minus the rapping.

 ELVIN J. HOYT II is a fifteen-year-old kid out of South Central L.A. He is a future rapper/producer, an artist, and Kanye's biggest fan.

 ARLYN JIMENEZ is a faithful daughter who loves her mother. She is strong, beautiful, and intelligent . . . no one can put her down.

 BRIAN JIMENEZ spends his time photographing the unnoticed beauty in life.

COURTNEY JOHNSON is a seventeen-year-old girl interested in all things beautiful. Those who know her know that she is full of fun, optimism, and charisma. She also loves purple! She will grow up to pursue acting, singing, and in her spare moments, she will write plenty of poetry.

 LA SHANEÈ KING is a special writer because she uses her own experiences as an African American to enhance her writing. She is extremely open-minded and understanding and enjoys helping out her community.

SADE LEEPER-SMITH is a regular sixteen-year-old girl, who most people would call crazy, silly, clumsy, or just not all there. But she is just a girl doing her thang. She is a dancer, and her future plans are to go to Spelman College and pursue a dancing career.

MALLORY LESTER is a goofy and loud, yet smart and open-minded, Afro-American. She is the one that they never saw coming. With that said, she is determined to stay in the spotlight.

 MIKESHA MINGO is a sixteen-year-old basketball princess. She dedicates her personal narrative to her grandmother, Julia Walker, and gives a special shout-out to anyone who reads this and knows her.

CANDICE MONROE was born in Los Angeles, California. She enjoys playing piano, violin, singing in the church choir, and playing tennis and basketball. One of her major goals is to graduate from high school and go on to college while majoring in performing arts.

 DANIEL MONROE was born on September 29, 1990, in Los Angeles, California and enjoys

179

drawing, movies, and video games. He plans to major in art at one of the UC colleges. He really enjoyed participating in this writing project and hopes that everyone enjoys reading this book as much as he enjoyed contributing to it.

JACQUELINE MORENO has a big name and a big family—four boys and six girls. She is understanding and kind, and she enjoys fun with her family and friends.

NOEL MUÑOZ is seventeen years old and was raised in Inglewood, California. He is a football player who loves watching basketball and baseball. The three people he looks up to are his parents, Maria and Francisco Muñoz, and his favorite basketball player, Kobe Bryant.

 ISHMAEL NAYLOR is a laid-back, music-loving guy with dreams of being a producer and getting his music out there. Some of his favorite artists include Tupac, Nas, and Naughty by Nature.

 RANDY PALACIOS is a member of the Ánimo Inglewood basketball team. He was the captain of the JV team this year and played varsity. He is determined to do anything.

 GERALDIN PONCE would like to dedicate her piece to her mother and father, who have been great inspirations in her life. She hopes to see the day the Dodgers win their next World Series.

 TERRELL POOLE is a young black man who aspires to be a director. He is someone with intelligence, integrity, and intensity. He is the American Dream.

ZOROBABEL PRUNEDA is a caring, sweet, sixteen-year-old girl who likes to make people laugh and smile. She's very optimistic about life and expects nothing but the best for her future. She can be a dork sometimes, but for the most part she's lovable.

 ROCIO SAMUEL-GAMA was born in Los Angeles and loves to travel and play all types of sports (except football). She hopes to one day attend UCLA, become a doctor, and make a difference.

 SHAWNA STEPHENS aspires to become a professional wedding planner. She enjoys sewing, singing, and writing poetry and songs. She has much love for her family, friends, Kobe Bryant, and the Lakers forever.

CHRISTINA STEWART is a sixteen-year-old writer with dreams that never meet the horizon. She plays varsity basketball for Ánimo and she has been playing the piano for thirteen years. God has blessed her with many desirable qualities, and she makes a sincere effort to use them to the best of her ability.

 ELIZABETH TRUJILLO is a funny, outgoing young lady who loves to spend time with her friends. She enjoys watching movies and loves to read.

 DEJUANNA WALLACE is a down-to-earth person with a logical but skeptical view of life. She is funny, accepting, and a nice person.

 ARIS WHITE is sixteen years old and in the eleventh grade. She wants to further her education at Howard University and to major in psychology. She enjoys reading, writing, listening to music, watching TV, shopping, and drooling over her soon-to-be-husband, 50 Cent, just like a regular teenage girl.

 CHRISTEN WILLIAMS is a going-on-sixteen-year-old, fun-loving type of gal who has her head on somewhat straight. Seriously, she does like to seek thrilling endeavors and opportunities.

ACKNOWLEDGMENTS

Rhythm of the Chain required months and months of work from the students at Ánimo Inglewood Charter High School, as well as from the teachers, 826LA tutors, and our volunteer editorial board. The students spent an astounding amount of time on their essays, making sure that they were the best that they could be—they gave up Saturdays, time after school, even some of their spring break to work on this book.

On behalf of 826LA, I would like to thank the three English teachers at Ánimo Inglewood who spearheaded this project: Annette Gonzalez, Allen Monroe II, and Melinda Viren—this book would not have been possible without their dedication to the students and to this book. We must also acknowledge the great support that they received from Steve Barr, founder of the Green Dot Charter Schools, and principal Cristina de Jesus.

826LA began this project in early March 2005 with the express knowledge that we needed to have a book published by June 2005. With the enthusiasm of our tutors and the hard work of the students, we always believed we could take on the impossible deadline. Tutors met regularly with students to review some eleven, twelve, even fifteen draft versions of short stories, poems, and plays—drafts that finally came together after intense and often emotional work sessions. The spectacle of tutor and student, elbow to elbow, working away and discussing every idea, word, and comma was inspiring to us all. The tutors' work was invaluable and they must all be mentioned here: Karen Ahn, Adam Baer, Shelby Benson, Rebekah Bradford, Ginny Brewer, Julie Bush, Loara Cadavona, Joanna Calo, Elizabeth Daniels, Amanda Davis, David Earle, Carol Gronner, Jori Finkel, Julie Golden, Lew Harris, Shelby Hiatt, Jenny Hontz, Jerry Jaffe, Herb Jordan, Mike Keeper, Soyun Kim, Jonathan Lababit, Dylan Landis, Douglas Lawrence, Sarah Lebo, Allison Lee, Genevieve Leone, Eileen Luhr, Matt Markwalder, Jamie Mayer, Tom McKenzie, Maria McNally, Ashley Merryman, Jean Miller, Kate Milliken, KaSondra Moore, Kristy Munden,

Susan Niedzwiecki, Will Richter, Tom Robertson, Jane Sprague, Claire Smith, J. Ryan Stradal, Lien Ta, Terena Thyne, Sobrina Tung, Diana Wendling, Jaime Wolf, George Wolfe, and Diane Wright.

The extraordinary student editorial board must be recognized for all the work that they did above and beyond writing—coming up with the title of the book, conceptualizing the cover, and attending many long meetings. They are: Cindy Ballón, Daniela Dowells, Allison Howard, Elvin S. Hoyt II, Sade Leeper-Smith, Rocio Samuel-Gama, Christina Stewart, Christen Williams, and Aris White.

Thanks must also go to our volunteer editorial board—professional writers and editors from the community—whose assistance was tireless: Adam Baer, Lynell George, Cara Haycak, Tami Mnoian, Jervey Tervalon, David L. Ulin, and Deborah Vankin. Anne Fishbein must be mentioned for her insightful lens and the beautiful photographs on the cover and throughout the pages; Michele Perez for creating the book's elegant design and devoting so many hours to its production; copy editors Sherri Schottlaender and Tami Mnoian for always making us look better. Thank you to Claire Smith, who provided an amazing amount of support to this project, and to Amber Early for taking on additional work while I concentrated on the book.

Extreme gratitude is due to Phil Jackson for the many hours he dedicated to this volume and its student writers. As the progenitor of the book's concept of "teamwork," Phil met regularly with the students and encouraged them to keep writing through the various drafts. After meeting every day through spring break, the students were rewarded with tickets to a Lakers game—we thank Phil Jackson and Jeanie Buss of the L.A. Lakers for arranging a memorable milestone in this project.

Lastly, a heartfelt thank-you to Nínive Calegari and Dave Eggers for paving the road for this book and lending their incredible expertise to this project.

I hope that you are inspired by the honest, insightful, and captivating stories in this collection.

Pilar Perez
Executive Director
826LA

826LA

ABOUT 826LA

826LA helps students, ages 6-18, with their writing skills, whether it is in the realm of creative writing, expository writing, or English as a second language. We offer free drop-in tutoring, afterschool classes, storytelling events, and assistance with student publications.

TUTORING IS AT THE HEART OF IT

Our method is simple: we assign free tutors to students so that the students can get one-on-one help. It is our belief that great advancement in English skills and comprehension can be made within hours if students are given concentrated help from knowledgeable tutor-mentors. We also offer tutoring in English as a second language.

FIELD TRIPS

We want to help our teachers get their students excited about writing, while also helping students to be better at expressing their ideas. We welcome teachers to bring their classes in for field trips during the school days. A group of tutors is on-hand at every field trip, whether we are helping to generate new material or revise already written work. Our most popular field trip is Storytelling & Bookmaking; the entire class works together with our tutors to create a story, along with illustrations, and each student leaves with his own book.

WORKSHOPS

Our tutors are experts in all different areas of writing: from comic books to screenplays to science fiction. That's why we're able to offer a wide variety of free workshops to students. One of our favorites so far, *ImagiNation: If I Were King or Queen . . .* allows students the opportunity to create their own country, replete with maps, flags and laws. Workshops are offered almost every day of the week, so sign up!

IN-SCHOOLS PROJECTS

The strength of our volunteer base allows us to make partnerships with Los Angeles-area schools. We coordinate with teachers and go en masse to a school and work with students in their classrooms. That is, if a history teacher at Venice High feels her students could use extra help revising a paper on violence in the Middle East, she could ask 826LA for support from ten tutors for her 2P.M. Thursday class. Tutors will arrive, ready to work one-on-one.

A BUSY SCHEDULE OF EVENTS

A busy schedule of guest speakers, classes, storytellers, and special events keep the building an active place. Please check www.826LA.org for our schedule of events.

For more information, please visit www.826LA.org, or email info@826LA.org.